THE WORKS OF HUO JINRONG: RAINBOWS, CLOVERS, LOTUS ROMANCE AND HEARTBEAT SONG

THIS BOOK IS WRITTEN BY HUO JINRONG

PUBLISHED BY ASIAN CULTURE PRESS

Published by Asian Culture Press LLC
1942 Broadway, Suite 314C,
Boulder, CO 80302,
United States

Published in the United States of America

First paperback edition September 2022

Introduction

This book named *The works of Huo Jinrong: Rainbows, Clovers, Lotus Romance and Heartbeat Song* is divided into the following four sections:

Rainbows are the personal stories, which relates to relationship, friendship and kinship.
Clovers are the family stories, which relates to trivial matters in daily life when the baby born.
Lotus Romance is a fantasy novel, which tells about the destiny and the mission of the lotus fairy and the human immortal.
Heartbeat Song is a romance novel, which tells about the love experience of the social anxiety sufferer and the affection cleanliness sufferer.

Writer: Huo Jinrong, university graduation, work in trade, from Shenzhen China, lived in the United States, and now settles in Switzerland.

Contents

Heartbeat Song

Rainbows
Rainbow One: (1) A Tree Full of Flowers

As a young adult, you are sitting quietly in the fast-moving train, while your heart has long drifted to the upcoming university life in the distance.

You are dreamily walking lightly, passing the scenery stroked by the rising sun along the road, obsessed with the gorgeous colors under the sunshine. Dusk is gradually approaching, the stars in the sky are a little lucid, and a bunch of bright moonlight touches your beating heart. Time passes through your soft face and stretches into the depths of your memory.

Fragrance wafts from a flat roof of the two-story farmhouse. A tree in the yard is full of flowers, constantly combing the poetry of its body. The words are hidden in the green leaves, patiently waiting for the flowers to bloom one after another. Constantly blooming, constantly chasing, where are the seeds that have sprouted. The thoughts flowed between the lines of the words, the tip of the pen dropped on the yellowed paper of the notepad, and the hopeful eyes were drawn into the silent ink.

Your father, who is busy in the poverty alleviation position, has a wrinkled dark face but a firm smile in the corner of his eyes, believing that his daughter has grown up. Your mother with graying hair, in addition to taking care of a large orchard with a good harvest, also needs to take care of your mental-ill uncle. The family's chatter at the dinner table reminded each other of their silent concern. Said to be uncle, in fact, he is more like a brother. He was the young son of your grandparents, born when they were old. The age difference was only a few years. Your parents don't want to talk more, but they just mentioned to you sadly that your uncle has suffered the double setbacks of employment and love.

You expect to step out a way, leave the high wall of calloused chains behind you, and bravely pursue a blue sky you've never seen before. Go out of the countryside, out of the town, out of the city, out of the province, away from the vitriol of some neighbors, and away from the sarcasm of some classmates.

A dazzling meteor, gently gliding across the boundless sky in the dark night, suddenly fell into the long river of time swept by the breeze. The dawn is approaching, when the train passes through the scenery of mountains and rivers. Your eyes wake up from the depths of memory and start to yearn for the blooming of flowers.

Rainbow One: (2) The Smell of Late Autumn

The freely university life has begun. Some of the roommates are busy in love, some are busy shopping together, but you bow your head in the pile of books.

The sky was washed by the icy rain last night. When you walked out of the dormitory building to catch up with the morning class, you could vaguely taste the smell of late autumn in the oncoming wind. On both sides of the stone-stairs road extending forward, the holly trees are carefully cultivated, and they are still working hard to grow green in the life.

A well-liked hometown fellow, he caught you walking with wind in the corner of the morning light, and hurriedly pulled you to greet you warmly. While you were responding hastily, you noticed a person. He was the roommate of your hometown fellow, a tall and elegant boy, with a sunny, clean and handsome face, like a warm spring sunshine, spilling into your gradually opening shy heart. No matter how many flowers bloom, no matter what the season is, just waiting for this beautiful encounter.

The winter snow is coming, fluttering like goose feathers. The sky is white, you from the South, which is the first time you have seen such a charming scene. Even sitting in the huge study room of library, your soul has quietly drifted out of the window to pursue the pure color one after another. The footsteps danced lightly, wading through the windless voice, picturesquely carved the traces of the ice and snow, and guarded the bright red heart in the green years.

The books full of notes were neatly put into the backpack from the wooden table with the scent of ink, and the library bathed in the ocean of knowledge was already in the distance. Looking back the footsteps you took in the snow, it was like the colorful spots in a pure white dream. Your thick eyebrows, big eyes and shallow red lips couldn't hide your smile. A little snowflake landed on the tip of your pretty nose, the moment you raised your eyes, you met him again, that clean and handsome face, hidden in the dark coat and hat, and the neat coat set off him even more outstanding. You both looked at each other without words, penetrating the thick cold breath.

Before the winter vacation and the Spring Festival, various colleges hold social activities. You simply dressed up and followed your roommates to join in communication from different clubs. You and him crossed the crowds one after another, seemed to cross the mountains and rivers one after another, just for the encounters that were silent but attracted to each other again and again. The most beautiful beatings lingering in the heart are folded into a poetic flower sea of mutual admiration, and the breeze of first love is silently inquiring about you and him.

Rainbow One: (3) A Rainbow of Hope

The spring rain was entangled outside the white window, while the cherry forest in front of the academy was in bloom, pink color, a little squeamish.

You want to plant a big tree with only branches. On the way forward every day, turn your life into green leaves. Colorful petals emerge from the branches. The beautiful song from the lark is among the rolling leaves. Gently, the wonderful figure of the butterfly comes from the strong fragrance of flowers.

In the quiet library, he sits next to you. There is a world growing in your heart. The bright sunshine falls from your thin shoulders to your heart, and it freezes into a clear white cloud. His blue shirt, your silver skirt, weaving a rainbow of hope, how beautiful.

In the old national university, time is as young as ever. Early summer has come. By the round pond on the North Campus, a few dragonflies are standing among the bright lotus flowers. Under the scorching sunshine, the cool breeze blows the lotus leaves sparkling. The school bus jumped and trotted around in circles. You knew what he was thinking in your heart, and he was walking towards you at the appointed time. The joy of seeing each other was better than the shinning lotus in the whole pond.

You heard that the snail noodle restaurant from the South opened, your friends avoided the smell that stimulated your taste buds, but you happily invited him to taste it together. In the cooking skills passed down from generation to generation, northerners like to eat pasta, and southerners like to eat rice. When the rice noodles are taken out from the boiling water and paired with sour and spicy bamboo shoots, crispy Yuba, fresh lettuce, fragrant river snail and broth, a taste from food heaven will permeate. He watched you graciously and emotionally as you swallowed the eight taels of rice noodle into belly. When the people around casted incredible surprise looking at you, the corners of his mouth unconsciously raised a charming arc of laughter. He reached out to help you wipe the sweat between your forehead hair.

The footsteps of the summer vacation are getting closer and closer. You and him are walking in the park, looking at the sky full of stars, holding each other's hands tacitly to establish a pure relationship, and telling each other about the summer vacation plan: You have begun to be competent for several tutoring jobs, and he is ready to arrive an internship in the street office of the super bustling city.

Rainbow One: (4) The Seeds of Dreams

Time passes through spring, summer, autumn and winter, with sun and moon changing along with the seasons. Diligent cultivation is sprinkled on the campus, with the seeds of dreams sowing in youth.

You step into the circle of his friends that he sincerely opened to you. People who are in love are accustomed to expecting each other to stay together for a long time, and longing for the wish to grow old together. Vibrant college students gather for outdoor outings on weekends, and talk about their ideal future under the sea of flowers surrounded by green mountains and clean waters.

The clear stream flows slowly from the field, the sound of the ding-dong spring wakes up the sycamore trees that are silently guarding the shore, and the stone-paved forest path extends forward from both sides of the sycamore trees. You looked down at the path under your feet, picked up two golden leaves that had just fallen down, placed one gently in his palms, and the other quietly nestled in yours. The two of you smiled at each other, holding hands lively to chase after the crowd that has gone away.

What is love? The college students around the gathering have their own answers. You compare it to a colored bicycle. He and you are the front wheel and the rear wheel of the bicycle respectively. You will kiss every inch of the front wheel's footprint, wait for him, pay attention to him, and worry about him. But on the road ahead, there are both unobstructed flat roads, thorny winding paths, and even rugged rocks and muddy potholes waiting. How to keep the bicycle of love going? It takes a concerted effort to keep the front wheel and the rear wheel from falling apart.

You meet the past of his life that he opened to you alone. A young diary that tells about the various thoughts of the teenager, and a pure picture album that records the growth stages of the years. The well-behaved text beats between your left and right eyes, and you look at the beautiful photos of him growing from a baby to an adult. You secretly marvel that he is a beautiful man blessed by God. Your heart longs for magic to take root and to carve your name and figure into his past.

Picking up the murmurs of the years, he takes you to revisit the school he attended since a child, ride the same school bus to the destination, eat the beef from the same shop, walk the same school playground, and see the familiar streets together. You have seen the grand scene of the city where he comes from, and you have seen the suburban villa where he lives. In the gentle breeze and drizzle, the vast twilight hides the bustle of people coming and going.

Rainbow One: (5) The Pictures

The busy study is gradually progressing, the tutoring job is getting better and better, and you are part-time foreign language translator at the same time.

With the income from the work effort, in addition to reducing some of the financial burden for the distant family, you also begin to be able to pay for the cost of traveling with him. The vastness of the motherland, the famous places and the historical sites that you can only see on TV, are the pictures of the world that you yearn to set foot on since your childhood.

The water town of Eastern Yangtze River is a dreamy fairyland. In the call of moonlit flowers, the courtyard is with holy beauty. By the riverside of the town tower where the lights are as day, you are playing windy tunes. At the strings of moving like water, it is his fingertips who dance under the fragrance of his sleeves. The ancient buildings with blue tiles and white walls are full of sunshine, mists and clouds drifted away, revealing the graceful mountains with undulating melody.

Heading to the red tour of Southern Revolutionary Base, you and him get into the clean and tidy slow train, to feel the slow movement of time outside the window. The noisy crowd in the city gradually faded away, replaced by the melodious cicadas in the mountains. The lush forest slowly retreated from the front, where a vigorous goshawk swept across the blue sky. The fields of hope are up and down, yet the Cole and peanut are flourishing all over the mountains. In the winding landscape, there is a simple vivid atmosphere. The people who get on the train along the way, with various kinds of luggage and crops stacked on the frame, can laugh and chat together whether they know each other or not.

In the ancient ethnic villages of Western Region, those colorful exquisite houses carved over time are located on the edge of the mist-shrouded mountains and forests. You and him, who are full of curiosity, listen carefully to the detail explanation of the local guide, and search the historical footprint behind each myth and legend. In the century-old shop, where decorated full of flowers, buy a pair of five-color sachets to wear on body. Crisp and loud folk songs have come from the corridor, crossing the river of time and coming from the other side.

The thousand-year-old temple is lonely standing in Northern Desert, with the lonely camel bell crossed the mighty sand sea and came to the chanting of the sutras that struck the wooden fish. You don't understand why the endless stream of believers kneel to the statue, with pious obsession in their eyes and unforgettable words in their mouths, all for power and wealth. He was smile and pointed you to the patio with a pool of coins, but unexpectedly you grabbed a handful of coins and pulled him to run quickly.

Rainbow One: (6) This Vast World

The hands of the clock become more and more hurried in the ticking sound, while the footsteps of time have long gone away in silence.

After many years of study, you finally meet the graduation. It is the unique fate to be able to meet in the old national university in this vast world, to become roommates living together and classmates studying together. How many springs, summers, autumns and winters you have worked and studied hard, and how many sun, moon and stars you have been pursuing ahead, in order to grow wings for the dreams in heart and welcome the wind and rain after stepping in society. At the farewell ceremony, everyone took pictures with each other, said goodbye to their mentors, then went their separate ways. You quietly wiped the tears from your eyes when no one was paying attention.

Your job-hunting journey is bumpy, and countless resume letters are thrown out like a rock. However, his job search seems to be smooth sailing. He passed the multiple examinations of government departments very early, and before graduation, he has confirmed that he will hold a post in the city office of Special Zone. You have submitted your resume countless times, interviewed for positions countless times, but failed countless times. Your anxiety is getting harder and harder to hide, and your frustration is frantically eating away at the fighting spirit.

Fortunately, the vitality like weeds is your characteristic, and you stand up again as many times as you are knocked down. You finally find a job where he is. Although there is a long internship period, you are very relieved, and the anxiety in your heart is blown away by the joyful moment. He is also very happy for you. When you squeeze out of the crowd, you can see him waving to you in the distance.

He carefully brings you to his parents and relatives, formally introduces you to them, and tries to integrate you into this important circle of connections. It's a pity that things are contrary to the wishes. You can't leave a qualified impression to his family. They don't like your student-look temperament, and they don't like your mental-ill family background. From these high-ranking people, there are indifference in their smile, which makes you hardly breathe.

In the splendid dining environment, the elegant and soothing background music is continue, however it can't lighten up the heavy moods of you and him at all.

Rainbow One: (7) Floating Life

A relationship that has been hurt by a sharp knife is like a young greenhouse flower that loses its protective layer and is easily damaged by frost.

The handsome and excellent young man with a wealthy family has become the ideal object of those girls for chasing after. Looking at him in his work and life, he frequently encounters those girls who take the initiative to show him love. Many of them are more outstanding than you, and their statuses are also more noble than you. Their unclear phone calls and ambiguous messages make you nervous.

In daily trivial matters, you quarreled with him constantly. He thought you became more and more unreasonable, while you thought he became less and less secure. Having seen the best side of each other, as well as the ugliest side of each other, you finally realized that the distance between you and him is getting further and further. Since he is already closer to someone else, you think it is time to separate.

But when you are used to a person, it is a difficult task to separate when you say separation. After several years of getting along day and night, to wipe each other out from life is like taking the oxygen away from breath. Since someone must play the negative role, this time is your turn to do it. When you moved the last luggage out of the house that contained his atmosphere, he stood behind you and kept begging you to stay. For that moment, you really want to be back with him, but you know this is not the future. You are sensitive, you feel inferior, then you choose to escape. Even after many years, the sobbing face when he watched you leave is unforgettable, no matter what, and will always be fixed in your mind.

At the end of the long internship period, due to the diligent performance of non-stop overtime, the multinational corporation decided to transfer you to an overseas job. Sitting in a small position by the window of the plane, you look at the territory that is far away, all the lands and seas have long since disappeared. The rolling clouds and mist are covered with a fictional story, and you came out of the birthplace with a wet body, holding a ray of light condensed by the Meditation.

Floating life is like a dream, personal trace is like smoke, yet it cannot stand the expectation. Can't escape, can't avoid, can't go back, and can't come out, leaving a vague figure.

Rainbow Two: (1) A Wandering Ghost

Oh, life, how to describe it? You are like a distressed painter, picking up the crayon in your hand, but it is difficult to draw the whole picture. If life is a wonderful all-encompassing balloon, and you're just a tiny speck of dust floating inside. Severe winters and harsh summers, rising sun and setting sun, indifference and enthusiasm, light and darkness, are all what life looks like. You should be happy to be able to witness the myriad of manners in life with your own eyes.

In the middle of the night, on both sides of the silent city streets, there are long road lamps emitting a cold and yellow light. In the entrepreneurial building with countless small offices, you have turned into a wandering ghost, your pale and thin fingertips are rapidly typing on the keyboard, your eyes are bloodshot after staring at the computer screen for a long time, and your freshly washed clothes are on the computer case for the heat to dry. In the corner of the office is a military-style folding bed, and in another corner near the bathroom, is your simple furniture, a well-organized little world, with everything you have.

The thunder rumbled outside the window, as well as the winter rain was falling, under the hazy sky, washing the turbid air of the city that was fleeing everywhere. Once upon a time, the sky in your hometown was also full of dark clouds, lightning and thunder. On that stormy night, the kind grandparents sat under the eaves of the window and told the old stories in a soft voice. You and your brother sat beside them. The fascinated little heads have long forgotten the fear of the world outside the house.

The rivers flow, the fields are flat and wide, and the rushing waterfalls run straight down on the steep rocks, where the mountains are high and the peaks are undulating. In the open forest with green trees, cheerful birds sing among the flowers and leaves. You love the hometown with the blue sky, as well as there are family members you care.

You have the goal of fighting for life, and the future of your family is the driving force for your hard work. No matter how heavy the darkness of the night is, or how dazzling the daytime of tomorrow is, as a ghost wandering in the urban space, you have no time to feel pity for yourself. Before dawn, you need to seize the time to get into the single bed and rest. The city gets busy during the day, and you turn back into a normal human getting ready to work.

You who have changed back to a human seem to be full of youthful vigor and vitality, as you are constantly striving to move forward on the thorny entrepreneurial road.

Rainbow Two: (2) The Rising Sun

Summer has passed. The city's cicadas are no longer screaming on the branches of the willow trees. The leaves are falling, the flowers are floating, and the sanitation workers in the streets are still working hard. The suffocating wind blowing to the face, you can vaguely feel the cool. Why the paces are in hurry? Is it in pursuit of the habitat for the wandering heart?

It is neither the light of the rising sun in the morning, nor the bright moon hanging high in the night sky, but the trust and affirmation of the customer on the other side of the ocean, the orderly business exchanges, and the continuous growth of orders, can give your startup company a new look and grow gradually. Your figure is busy in the receiving and dispatching warehouse full of items, and the trucks pulling in and out are constantly flowing.

The customer, a mysterious Jewish businessman, started out as sporadic email exchanges, constantly asking for design revisions, arranging for sample redoes, and negotiating with suppliers. Countless staying up all night and countless striving, finally let you see the dawn when the order is confirmed. You deeply realize that all your efforts may be fruitless, but the success you deserve is never born out of nothing.

This Jewish businessman, like a rare dawn star appeared in your ordinary life, leads you to knock on the new door of the business jungle. You shake the new feathers of your body, hold the seeds of hope in your mouth, fly through the busy sea of people, split a piece of territory that belongs to you in the vast jungle covered with mountains and plains, and put the seeds into the open space with your claws. Mud nest, doused with silent sweat. Looking forward to the coming year, the seeds of hope are in the soil of your territory, where spring is full of flowers, summer is full of rice, autumn is full of fruits, and winter is warm as usual.

Your world isn't full of company orders and customer merchandise, where family members are always in important places. In the dense schedule, there are always notices about the academic success of your brother and the health and longevity of your grandparents. You don't want to stop combating, because there are roaming beasts everywhere in the business jungle, you must be alert to the winding roads, and you must keep your eyes open and hone your sharp skills.

If you are reluctant to make progress or stay complacency, the beasts of the jungle will open their sharp claws from the darkness, gnaw and drink the blood of your limbs.

Rainbow Two: (3) The Fleeting Year

Through spring flowers and autumn moon, summer rain and winter snow, your life is on the wheel of experiencing the warmth and coldness of the world, and another year has passed. The feeling for the Spring Festival in your heart, because you are concerned about your family in the hometown, has become the warmest color in the fleeting year, which is transformed into the bright stars and a beautiful moon.

Neighbors from the East come to chat with your grandparents. You quietly watch their lips and teeth. The vivid muscles of their faces are performed heartily in the flying foam, and their throats are up and down. You cautiously pick up the words they left on the ground. It turns out that their young grandson they often mention, visited them in a luxury imported car with a dazzling body actually like a salted fish, driven from the head of the street to the end of the alley, publicizing about the uselessness of education.

Neighbors from the West also come to chat with your grandparents. What do they want to show off? It turns out that their most beautiful granddaughter who just grew up has been proposed by a big boss from HK. During the Spring Festival, they will hold an extravagant celebration. The more they talked, the more excited they became, and the gold bracelets in their hands made you feel dizzy. They try to persuade you, it is useless for a girl to educate too much, and it is better to rely on beauty to find a rich man.

Your grandparents are reasonable people, honest and modest, and only hope that their grandchildren will live a safe and happy life. After graduation, your brother finally gets a stable job in the city not far from the hometown, and you use the savings you have accumulated over the years to buy them a new ideal house in the city.

The neighbors from the East heard that you were buying a new house in the city, yet they no longer like to chat with your grandparents. But you don't know when, rumors from them began to flow out to the streets and alleys, slandering your brother involved in some dirty deals to earn the black money for buying a house.

The neighbors from the West heard that you were buying a new house in the city, yet they also no longer like to chat with your grandparents. In private, they are in groups of three or five, telling others everywhere that you are for behaving a bad conduct and not abiding the women's morality, only then can you afford to buy a house. You are so angry that you want to set these people on fireworks and blow them up.

Rainbow Two: (4) A Warm Beacon

You are a person who cherishes yourself, and your life will not be overshadowed by the hateful words of others. That group of self-righteous civilized people, in the name of adhering to correct moral teachings, always talk about the rotten clichés that have long decayed from the root. They take pleasure in playing the role of God's way, judging those who do not meet their eyes, are heretics or traitors, and need to be purified or wiped out.

They call you the savage that didn't follow the rules they've worked out for cheating. You don't care too much the gossip that goes around, but when you hear about the savage, you take a moment from the cracks of your busy working career to consider the meaning of the word.

You, who moved the eyebrows lightly, groaned deeply in your heart, you have never been advertised as a civilized person, and you will not be a civilized person in your bones. You didn't bury your pure desires in a sly and pretentious posture. Looking up at the sky and the earth, you see the mountains are high and the clouds are light. You care about whether your pursuit is focused enough, rather than letting those irrelevant thoughts contaminate your mind.

You admit that when you were a child, you once peed and pooped in the open wild hill, but you always dug a hole in advance, after done, then covered it with thick soil and green weeds. Those people who claim to represent civilized models, in addition to their passion for gossip behind, they don't even flush the public toilets after peeing and pooping, making the clean and bright public toilets smell bad.

The development of your company has not been smooth sailing. You have encountered factories that detained your company's quality inspectors but because of their substandard products. You have encountered agents who sent rogues to block your company's door because you don't cooperate with them. You have encountered customer representatives who are delusional about taking advantage of your company's female employees, and that Jewish businessman has taught you how to be smart.

Your heart is not frozen. When someone gives you the care silently and sincerely, like a warm beacon to guide you on the way through the boundless darkness, with the accumulated years of getting along, the empty feeling in heart will be always gone, blooming bright flowers in life.

Rainbow Two: (5) The Other Side of the Ocean

The impetuous downtown is bustling. You pick up the looks that you have forgotten in the river of time. It is rare to meet the fate in the silent years. The breeze from the other side of the ocean is coming slowly, blowing the colorful flowers of rainforests with rippling water. You are dressing up in front of the bright mirror by gorgeous clothes and graceful appearance. Your skirts are fluttering in the wind.

Beautiful scenery, picturesque fireworks, and an extra elaborate engagement ring on your slim finger. The Jewish businessman set off from the long island on the Atlantic coast with full affection, crossed the turbulent Pacific Ocean, and appeared with a tall decent figure in front of you.

You open the life book in your hand, it is a brand new page of ink paintings that have not yet been filled with color, and he will write the poems of this page together with you. The tacit of understanding each other, placed a bunch of elegant and rich bamboo, ordered a box of overflowing sandalwood, and held a roll of magical books. In the poetry and beautiful sentences, in the ceramic and jade moonlight, lightly close your eyes, and piece together the many years of fantasy encounters into a circulating star.

He went to visit your grandparents with you. The language barrier did not prevent him and your grandparents from having a sincere conversation. After the long stay, say goodbye to your wonderful family, arrange the affairs of the company properly, and you are sent by your brother to the bustling airport. From then on, you will fly into the clouds.

The world on the other side of the ocean is so novel. Those budding emotions hidden in your heart are like many tender goose yellow beans sprout, breaking through the thick soil and galloping under the uneasy and unfamiliar sunlight. You need to adjust the focal length of your emotions, use your inner lens well, and seriously capture the appearance of the new life you are experiencing. Under the blue sky and white clouds, the sea breeze blowing to the face, the villas are one after another on the island, not far from each other, quiet and peaceful, as well as far-reaching.

The family members have their own estates. Although his parents are quite old, they still love to travel around by the stylish convertibles. His ex-wife and children live in a large castle-like house, with beautiful gardens that are cared properly by dedicated servants. As a Jew, he married early and divorced early. The children born by his ex-wife are about ten years apart in age from you. Although it is unlikely to get along well, it can also avoid disturbing each other. Your daily focus becomes practicing traditional kosher rules, which is a headache for the worldly you.

Rainbow Two: (6) Clouds in the Sky

Living a quiet life, you think life should be like this. Your family is well, your career is successful, and you never want to encounter unexpected storms.

When your brother was in love, the girl was met through a matchmaker. Her behavior was honest and kind, which coincided with your brother's warmth personality. People often think that young persons are in love for the first time would have large or small conflicts, sometimes impulsive fists and feet, sometimes intense bickers. It is rare for your brother them to have no quarrels. The two naturally entered into the marriage gate and began an ordinary life of mutual support.

That nerdy boy, who used to follow behind you, who used to get protection from you, has finally grown into a real man, able to build a new family on his own, and start a new journey in life to raise children. At a traditional Chinese wedding, watching your brother and his happy lady in red wedding outfits pour tea and wine to the elders in a festive atmosphere, you can't help but moisten your eyes.

Time flies, Clock slips through the years, and a cold wind with the smell of frost and snow knocks down a few clouds in the sky. You remember that just after the New Year's Day, the company's personnel returned to work one after another. During the meeting, your mobile phone was switched to vibration but kept receiving calls from afar. Your heart was inexplicably panicked. The sad voice of your brother came from the other end. Said that Grandpa is dying, and asked if you can come back to see him for the last time?

You open your mouth, but can't speak, your voice is stuck in your throat. You hear other people's concerned sounds from time to time, however you can't hear clearly. Your head is dizzy, tears running down your pale cheeks. You are afraid of hitting death! How can your good grandpa suddenly die? You want to remember his kind face forever in your mind, so you choose to escape like a coward clown.

Your grandpa's death brought a fatal blow to your grandma. It looked normal on her face, but her whole soul already followed your grandpa. She would still put dishes and chopsticks for your grandpa at the dinner table, and would talk to herself to the air, as if your grandpa never left her. Another year just after the New Year's Day, you received the same call from your brother that Grandma is dying. The two elders who have lived for nearly ninety years die in the same way.

Rainbow Two: (7) The Fate Gone

Life does not follow the planned track after living in a foreign country. You both cross two continents and oceans all year round, and problems arise one after another.

Business jungles are like battlefields. Even though he is the Jewish businessman who have experienced hundreds of battles and made huge fortunes before his twenty, he encounters unpredictable landslides in the dark jungle. Excessive delegation of power to the cooperation Group's partners, he suffered fraud and betrayal, while ended up with debts and frozen funds. The court summons swept through him like bullets that had passed through his bones, battering him with deadly wounds all over his body.

This poised, high-ranking man, who now speaks to you with sorrow eyes and dejected words, can't give you and the future family the glory and wealth as he gave to his ex-wife and the existing children. He is worried all the time the young you will one day complain about him, hold a grudge against him, and leave him. You want to say that you are not such a person, but there is a voice from the bottom of your heart: you can't change the habit of eating pork and eating lobster.

You sold out the most expensive large-scale commercial houses in the harbor real estate, while your friends who knew you said that you were too stupid. Large sums of money fly across the ocean. He didn't expect you come to rescue him without hesitation, and his parents, ex-wife and children looked up to you. When you were about to return the engagement ring with both hands, he didn't take it, but he turned his face away so that you wouldn't notice his painful state, then explained in a hoarse voice that the engagement ring was also worth a house, and maybe one day it could save you from danger.

The unpredictable business situation and the sudden increase in raw materials and labor force have made many customers look for business opportunities in other countries. It is as if your company was the leaked house while it was raining overnight. Several containers of products suddenly had an accident. In the end, he tried his best to help you deal with it properly, so as not to lose everything.

Later, he did not remarry, moved back to the big castle-like house to be with his ex-wife as brother and sister, and his children were happy to see it. Other houses and places were vacated, which he turned to the cause of supporting the Jewish religion and developing children's education. Later after later, he always inquired about your situation intentionally or unintentionally, and helped you out of obstacles quietly. However, if the fate is gone, the life has to find another beginning to start all over again.

Rainbow Three: (1) Plain Face

During the holidays, you are too lazy to get movement. You still haven't stepped out of the door, but stayed in the bed motionless, with a mess of hair like a chicken coop. The dark circles under your eyes from staying up late are like panda eyes. A cell phone on the bedside table is buzzing. You don't have to look at it to guess that it's a text message from your parents urging you for blind date.

You reach out and rub your dry plain face, slap a few times to wake yourself up a bit, then evoke the memory of the failed blind date. He was an excellent man working in a state-owned bank, introduced by your aunt's family. He was three years older than you, dressed in a suit and leather shoes. The two of you are sitting in a cafe, and he is holding your personal information, which is boring. It is more like a job interview than a blind date. When finally leaving the venue, you both wave goodbye to each other, then there is no more.

Seeing you haven't responded for a long time, your parents are calling urgently. You want to bury your head in the duvet and you want to be like an ostrich, pretending that you can't hear the sound, but the uninterrupted ringing makes you sleepless. You had to bite the bullet and pick up the phone to answer. It turned out that the blind date this time was an IT man working in the Aviation Bureau, who was also three years older than you and a distant relative of your aunt's family.

Unsurprisingly, this blind date ended in failure again. He is looking for the ideal person who can carry on the family line according to the preferences of his parents. It doesn't matter whether there is love or not, and your conditions do not seem to meet the ideal person for him. You listen to your inner voice, if a relationship built without love is like a dangerous territory where a time bomb is buried, and you are afraid that only the bones may remain.

In order to let your parents don't worry, you assume that you have a stable relationship, so you do not need blind dates for you in the future. In fact, you are neither keen on the marriage life, nor are you a person who loves to seek a partner, and the fate does not favor on you too.

If a person does not rely on the Internet, the number of people she will contact with in her life may be limited to campus, workplace, and the circle of relatives and neighbors. Coincidentally, you received a friend invitation from a famous global social platform. Since both have common connections, trying to become friends seems not too bad.

Rainbow Three: (2) The Waterfalls from the Peaks

After agreeing to add the friend invitation, you turn around and forget about it. You still do whatever you need to do every day, eat and drink, sleep when you need to sleep, work when you need to work, and don't stay up late but continue to stay up late. The same steps are repeated almost every day.

You're becoming more and more socially distant. Maybe you're a miser who doesn't want to put in the time and energy to run the chores that you don't have to do. You prefer to be alone, you also enjoy the passage of time alone, and you have a dialogue with your own heart. It is an intimate fusion of richness and blandness. In your space-time dimension, it seems that there is no meaning for loneliness.

Check your mobile banking account, work hard for some more time, accumulate the deposits, and you can pay off the mortgage, then the burden on your shoulders can finally be lifted. You have always been so tireless in planning your life. Since you were a kid, you have developed the habit of planning short-term and long-term goals. No matter whether you can get your wishes or not, it is better to have a plan than a mess. Anyway, you have formulated a life outline. Watch, you can continue to be lazy again with peace in mind, then continue to next year when it fails to materialize at the end of this year.

You want to invest in a small store, but what should you sell? You stand in your house and start rubbing your forehead in serious thought. How about selling milk tea? It is simple enough, but you don't like pearls, especially you feel that throwing away half a cup of pearls after drinking the cup of milk tea is a waste of food. How about selling cold noodle? As a typical southerner, yet you like northern snacks. You fell in love with the taste of cold noodle and gluten when you were in university. The side dish of cold noodle, fresh cucumber, can also be used to make a handmade mask, which saves more money!

You go to the balcony with a wide view, seeing the sky is clear for thousands of miles. It was still a strong storm just now. The forests and the mountains are faintly visible in the opposite canyon and the waterfalls from the peaks are rushing to merge into the streams and rivers next to the community park, happily running to the sea ahead.

The laptop placed on the desk, with the open mailbox sounding a reminder. You approach the desk with curiosity, and wonder who is writing to you?

Rainbow Three: (3) The Same Answer

You stared blankly at the computer screen for about half an hour, with unpredictable emotions beating in your heart. Do you want to reply to this letter from a stranger? Although you have been adding him for some time, you did not expect that this global workplace platform can make friends.

Sure enough, he is a typical Englishman, since he likes to ask you about the local weather in the opening talk. What can you say? He asks you the weather question every day, and you have to reply the same answer every day. After all, you're on the southern coast, where typhoons are common occurrences.

You two really got to know each other from a very large typhoon. It was with the strongest wind force reaching level 15. Under such extreme weather, every household in the community closed their doors and windows tightly and hid in their comfort zone tremblingly. Through the sealed transparent glass window, you look at the world outside in horror. There are dark clouds, lightning and thunder, and the darkness is overwhelming. This is the rhythm of the doomsday!

He, who was far away, was actually concerned about you encountering this typhoon. The crisp ringing of the mobile phone rang and stopped, stopped and rang. You stretched out confused hands from the blanket rolled up like a pile of elephant dung to fumble around on the bedside table, then drowsily pressed the answer button. What came to your ears was the elegant and pure London noble accent. The magnetic voice was patiently explaining: because he didn't hear from you, he called you to ask if everything is okay? You stayed home for these a few days hibernating like a sheltered turtle and apologetically told him that you weren't online.

After meeting a productive conversational buddy, your daily trajectory has changed a little. He is accustomed to video chat with you, so that you can understand his daily life and let you know his office environment. Even driving to golf on free days, he can talk to you for most of the time.

You and him are getting to know each other more and more, and you don't even realize that you are used to sharing the little things in your life with him. Even if it is trivial, you will tell him about it. For example, in the public elevator room of the community, you encountered a bad child with a scooter heavily banging on the floor numbers, you kindly tried to stop him, but you were scolded by the bad child's mother and grandma. He later comforted you to suggest the administrator to deal with it next time.

Rainbow Three: (4) Golden Ripples

One day, you received a call from his best friend to tell you about his sudden fall on the golf course. The examination at the hospital was not optimistic. He was very likely to be diagnosed with ALS. His best friend hoped that, in his limited life, you would be able to find time to visit him.

You have hardly noticed any news about ALS. This is the first time you have heard the word ALS since you were so far, but the fear of it has been deeply branded in your mind. You hurriedly searched the Internet for what is ALS? What symptoms will the patient have? Can it be cured? At the end, you find out in despair that this is one of the five major terminal diseases in the world. It cannot be cured at all!

He hasn't called you back for days, yet you still write and text him as usual. Talk about things around you, talk about trivialities, talk about the projects you are arranging for business trips, and talk about you will definitely come to see him. You hope him to cheer up, and you hope him not to be lost in your life.

The direct international flight is flying fast around half the earth, the rolling clouds and sea fog are boundless, where the horizon of the sky is filled with golden ripples. You sit quietly in the seat with the safety belt fastened, tossing and turning, sleepless in the middle of the night, looking through the autumn water inside your eyes and the seasons change outside your heart.

The work at hand is finished, and you can't wait to drive to your intended destination. He made an appointment with you to meet at a local high-end restaurant with a century-old heritage. When you see his driver carefully help him down the car door, your heart is piercing and hurt. It is a dazzling but cold cane. A year ago, he was still a healthy man with extraordinary vigor. How did he suddenly reach the fragile condition that he had to walk with a cane? You wish to remove the ALS from his body, to eliminate and wipe out this incurable demon that has tortured him.

He sees you rushing out to meet him, with an irresistible relief on his face, back to his wit and joy, setting aside the pain of illness for the time being. Each piece of exquisite western knives makes you accustomed to showing embarrassment that you don't know how to start. He will give you a warm smile by your side, and patiently explain the usage of each piece of the tableware. The happy atmosphere of the conversation stretches under the soft light, and the evening breeze without pain roams freely in the city.

Rainbow Three: (5) The Greening Grass

The second time you see him, it's another year, but he can't walk on foot anymore and can only move around in a wheelchair. His driver was a kind and hospitable guy who waited early at the arrivals hall exit of the international airport and kept introducing you the city along the way.

His home is an intelligent manor house. As soon as you arrive outside the garden, the gate would automatically open. The driver helped you bring your luggage into the hall on the first floor before leaving. The family nanny put down the kitchen work and walked downstairs to ask if you needed help. You were about to say no trouble, but he had already arranged everything for you. There was his happy voice from upstairs, and the family nanny helped you to put the luggage in your guest room on the top floor.

You wanted to go into the opening room on his floor and give him a big hug. But after long-distance flight trips, the whole person has been infected with invisible germs in different public places, which is harmful to his condition. When friends meet to say hello, go to bath and change clothes before going downstairs to catch up. He tells you that he had to quit his job as the CEO of a financial institution, since he was no longer competent in his position.

Because of the jet lag, you sat on the sofa beside him and snored while you accompanied him for a long conversation. He watched you languidly sleeping in peace. In order not to disturb you, he quietly instructed the family nanny to cover you with his precious collection of the floral blanket.

When you woke up, it was already afternoon. The family doctor who came into view was carrying out daily nursing matters for him. You watched silently from the side, with the sadness in your heart for the impermanence of life. However, he was worried about whether you were bored when you woke up, and cast an inquiring look at you.

The smart doorbell rang. His best friend walked in. This is a handsome black man with a high nose, white teeth, and a clean smile on his face. During the chat, you learn that the black friend's great-grandfather was also a great person whose portrait is kept in the local National History Museum. The family doctor said he was in good shape and could go for a walk. He wanted to go back to the golf course he frequented. You and his best friend carried him in the wheelchair, the three of you chatted and laughed, and walked to the place where the flowers were blooming and the grass was greening.

Rainbow Three: (6) The Belonging of Souls

You embark on the trip to see him. This is the third time you've been on the same non-stop flight, eating the same airplane food. The world outside the clouds, in the azure sky, is ethereal and quiet, with water moon and mirror flowers. You have thousands of thoughts, that the belonging of souls fall in the pure land where muse growth.

It's a new year. The streets and alleys here are filled with the traditional atmosphere of Christmas. The wind was cold, snowflakes were flying, and as far as the eyes could see, there was a vast expanse of white scenery. The lake adjacent to the garden is not as clear as it used to be. On the balcony of the manor house, snowmen in Christmas costumes are piled up. His physical condition became worse and worse, not only could his feet be unable to move, but his hands are gradually becoming immobile.

You're busy in the kitchen, all the festive ingredients are being prepared by the family nanny, and the two-shift family nurse has just arrived, moving in and out of his room next to the parlor. He has lost his ability to take care of himself, where he is lying on the lifting medical bed watching TV. He likes dialogue-style debate shows, and often says that this is a good way to train the brain: to absorb the wisdom and knowledge of others, to find flaws and loopholes in opponents, to defeat them by surprise.

He goes out of his way to pass on his insights to you while he can speak freely: people are usually only interested in things that are relevant to them, so when you talk to customers, be customer-centric and talk about topics that are relevant to them; everywhere, whether in life or at work, impulsive fighting or adding insults is not a smart approach, yet a witty sense of humor can subtly resolve many disputes.

Christmas and New Year gifts pass through the snow, from his two mothers and two nephews. He doesn't have much emotion for his mothers. After all, his parents from noble families divorced very early, and his father later remarried a BBC media executive as his stepmother. As for his two nephews, from his sister who divorced the banker. He introduces his two nephews with pride who are from the world's top universities and establish their own technology companies successfully.

The special environment created the special outlook on life, no wonder he never pursued marriage all his life. In the evening, the lights are bright all around, the black friend brings his favorite wine to spend the holiday with you and him, and he sighs with feelings: it is very precious to meet two confidants at the end of his life.

Rainbow Three: (7) Landscapes the Same but People Not

After several seasons of years, when the typhoons are dense again, international flights are forced to cancel. You could not do anything, only leaving it to the fate.

Noisy large supermarket, noisy people coming and going, added to your anxiety. The storm is coming, you need to buy daily necessities to fill the refrigerator, and prepare to stay long in the house. You received an emergency call during the way toward home with your heavy shopping bags.

You heard his hurried and indistinct voice on the other end of the phone. You slowed down and listened patiently, explaining to him that you would fly over to visit him immediately after the typhoon was over and the flight returned to normal. But you never imagined that this call was his last words with you in the world. After finishing the work around you, you tried to call him many times, yet no one answered. You thought he had fallen asleep, however, you were inexplicably uneasy.

An unfamiliar phone number sent you a text message, signed as his sister, to inform you that her brother is no longer alive,

and there are some matters in his will that need to be negotiated
with you. You read every word of the text message over and
over again, but your empty mind still can't believe it's a fact. In
a trance, you think of his black friend, hurriedly dialing the
phone, yet in silence, you get the same sad answer.

This is the fourth time you fly to his city, his country, but he
never sees you again. A funeral without any ceremony, just
you, his black friend and his sister at the manor house where he
once lived. The layers of lawyers' documents give you an
unbearable headache. You know that he would donate his body
and property to the ALS research institute. This is a topic he
discussed with you before his death. But you don't know that
he would leave a fund for you to support your study abroad and
living. In his videos and last words, he believes that this will
open a new stage in your life.

The thick envelope is handed to you. It is about that he still has
a wish need you help to realize. It was a plan which he did not
have the chance to carry out when he reached the end of his
life. He hopes that you can make up for his regrets and have an
unforgettable trip to the cities he suggested to broaden your
horizons. You follow the direction of his last wish, however,
when you return to the starting point again, it turns out: the
person is gone with the house empty; the landscapes remain the
same but people no more.

Rainbow Four: (1) The Scattered Stars

The subway whizzing past, crowded with people, you curled up at the end of the corner of the carriage, but you can't hide your tiredness in your formal dress. The push and pull coming towards you, there is no way to retreat. You close your eyes, and listen to the intense heartbeats nearby, where the pedestrians roar in silence. You see yourself as a tiny ant wandering in the body of this bizarre mechanical snake, crawling through deserted burrows.

The wind blows the clouds, and the clouds blow the rain. In the image of the cosmopolitan city, the sky is painted in a gray color, and those high-rise buildings block the sight. A sea grows out of your heart, with the waves beating on the silver beach. There is a fragrant island in the middle sea, a stone house lying on the island. The surrounding is vast, no trees grow, and no birds fly, only the sky and the sea.

Through the long blooming Redbuds, you dragged your heavy body back to the high-rise residence. When night falls, the temperature of the day cools down. You raise a pot of aquatic Ivy on the windowsill, the delicate and dripping leaves growing lushly. In the dark without sleepiness, you and Ivy accompany, leaning on the edge of the window, listening to the sizzling sound of the stars scattered in the grass.

You look for a bright flower, then you get a seed; you look for a clear spring, then you find a stream. Your soul won't speak nice words, but at least be honest with your heart. You don't want to be your own prisoner, tying your hands and feet to a senseless and false trial. Try it out, then break free from the invisible cage that imprisoned you. Look up at the wider sky, try to grow your wings, and soar stubbornly in the wind.

It is customary for the headhunting company to call to congratulate you on passing the rigorous interview of that famous international enterprise Group, and you will get the employment contract of the corresponding position as you wish. You thought there is little hope. Facing multiple blond interviewers, a few hours of question and answer, the feeling was like walking on thin ice.

The dark clouds in your heart dissipated, the sky washed by the rain, blue and clear, the fragrant green garden, blooming beautifully. A ray of dawn shines into the bitterness of reality, and a copper bell comes from a distant place. The road of life is tortuous, but it is always a forward practice.

Rainbow Four: (2) Modern Building

With a new career, a new work environment, you walk into the sixty-story modern building. This is a multinational Group headquartered in the European Union. Its business covers many fields around the world. The Asia-Pacific region focuses on production, and the North American region focuses on sales.

In the huge office space, employees of different ethnicities carry out daily affairs in their respective departments. The rising sun at nine o'clock rings the bell for a busy day of work. The manager of the human resource department, wearing a fresh and clean professional attire, will lead you to introduce the main persons in charge of each department one by one.

Your boss is a tall, blond, blue-eyed French man who is in charge of quality control of the supply chain in the Asia Pacific region. In fact, you met him in the question-and-answer session of the interview. And another tall, blond and blue-eyed man, the director of the human resource department, from Italy, has a cheerful personality and gets along well with your boss. You have been working in the new company for a while, yet there are no additional tasks other than arranging you to familiarize yourself with the SAP system.

Compared with your previous perception, the corporate culture of European-style company and American-style company is significantly different. In American company, one person is almost responsible for the workload of a team; while in European company, a team will be assigned to take charge of the workload of one person. American-style company doesn't care what to wear, even if come to work in T-shirt, short pant, and flip-flop; while European-style company requires business suits to be neatly worn, and even women's sandals with open toes are considered improper. When you get used to be busy, you come to work in a welfare-oriented European-style company, then you will have to take time to adapt it.

Since you have nothing to do, you take the curiosity to the surroundings that you will be familiar with, and your eyes see that: the British in the project department love afternoon tea; the Dutch in the purchasing department are tall and cold; the Spanish in the design department are good at football; the Singaporeans in the R&D department like to gossip; the Americans in the marketing department are rhetoric and talk eloquently; the Hongkongers in the finance department are preoccupied with their professionalism.

The coffee hall in the leisure area is a magical place. You can catch all kinds of people in the company. They come in groups of three or five to privately talk about their matters. A subtle division of the social circle, which is faintly visible, floats infinitely above the office.

Rainbow Four: (3) The Endless Flow

To expand the work capacity, you can't just sit and chat in the modern building with the air conditioner on. You are a person with the gene that is uneasy about the status quo in bones, and won't slip away the opportunity to participate in the supply chain management of the entire Group.

Following your boss's footsteps, you have traveled all over the factories and mastered the management standards of industrial science. The knowledge, experience and theoretical support obtained from practice are more valuable than the MBA certificate obtained by the high tuition fee. When you can be on your own, business trips at home and abroad gradually become a regular part of work. You see the endless flow of Asia-Pacific ports, dotted with container ships, rushing to the terminals around the world. You see the European and American airports where people and cars come and go, the conference meetings that follow one after another, and the dazzling array of products fill the shopping windows.

The advanced children's electric vehicle injects a new concept into education and entertainment, which is additionally equipped with intelligent early teachings, music playback, and multi-language learning. You have witnessed its whole process from design, research and development, mold opening, trial production, mass manufacturing, packaging according to demand, to warehousing and shipping. Long-term cooperative suppliers have the characteristics of wide base area, advanced production equipment, strong skilled workers, and efficient management team.

The multi-functional fully automatic wheelchair is a folding four-wheeled scooter for both medical and household use, providing indispensable convenience for the elderly or disabled people with limited mobility in life. Some of these combination parts come from different manufacturers. Such as lithium batteries, the most professional and powerful manufacturers are from mainland China. Such as wheels, due to the requirements of special customers, it can only use manufacturers from Taiwan, China.

About nursing products for infants and pregnant mothers, the hygiene requirements of the factory meet the highest standards. Visitors must wear protective clothing, shoes and hats, and perform comprehensive mechanical cleaning and disinfection before stepping into the production line for observation. In fact, many suppliers in Suzhou, China should be better than those in Korea.

About High-end fashion clothing, shoes and bags, from the runway to the public, designers need to absorb inspiration, often visit New York, Hong Kong, London, Paris, Milan and other most prosperous and most diverse global central cities, and integrate varieties of street photography for their own creativity.

Rainbow Four: (4) Where There Are People

Where there are people, there are right and wrong. The enterprise Group is like a small society. Whenever you see the gossip females whispering in the pantry or the corridor, you have a sense of oppression to run away.

They are really leisure and tasteless. If they cannot gossip at their will, probably they cannot stimulate happiness from their idle days. You are sitting in an office chair next to the computer desk, holding the yearly report of rejective products that has just been analyzed from the SAP system. The company regular meeting will be held soon, but phone calls and messages from suppliers are coming in from all directions. They hope you can help them to hide the rejective rate.

You can't help shaking your head, for these suppliers are not on the right track. Controlling product quality in place according to the established standards is the most worthy of core concern. It is short-sighted to let the defective products flow into the market. It will not only hurt the confidence of customers, but also not conducive to the development of the company brand, not to mention that the suppliers themselves will not be improved, and they may close the factory without orders. You suddenly feel that these suppliers are strangely similar to those gossip females, so you put them in the same category.

A person who has been single for a long time without a partner is easily regarded as an alien by these idlers around. You've just passed the aisle next to them, but their high-decibel squeaks force you to listen. It turns out that they are gossiping about your boss. No wonder they're so excited.

In fact, your boss knows that they often make irresponsible remarks and takes it as a deaf ear. It is nothing more than they are with poor mind who have no other interests and hobbies. They regard others' private affairs as jokes to fulfill their lonely lives, and use this to nourish their dry and empty hearts.

Memories drifted across the seas, clouds, mountains and rivers. You still remember that there was a departed relative in the hometown who devoted himself to studying I Ching and Herbal Compendium. Neighbors scolded him openly and secretly for being useless and unmarried, but how could they forget the past: they came to beg him for creating Feng Shui; he cured the incurable diseases for neighbors for free.

Rainbow Four (5): The Infinite Scenery

From the large demonstration hall in the activity area, there were cheers that were getting louder and louder, shaking the offices of various departments in confusion. What exactly is going on? Colleagues who went to find out, returned to their seats after half an hour and talked with relish. It turned out that the headquarters Group participated in the relevant public welfare activities of the United Nations, supported poor children back to school, donated stateless refugees, and implemented environmental and climate protection.

Everyone in the company who gets along day and night, usually looks up and sees each other, so naturally they can roughly understand each other's behavior. Those European and American who often party in cafes are more noisy and more fond of booing than those Asian-Pacific who get used to being silent in the workplace. Whenever you see a big man from Sicily followed by a small man who is inseparable, you can't help but think of the Godfather of the Mafia. Whenever you see an American who is chatting, accompanied by the British and Australians, you can't help but think of the Five Eyes Voldemort.

July and August are traditional holiday months. The company management has already flown to the tourist resort to enjoy the infinite scenery of the blue sky, white clouds and bright sunshine. You have nowhere to go, sit in the rocking chair at home, lean back against the bookcase, and immerse yourself in the pile of books.

Bunches of white flowers are placed in the empty office next door, as well as black and white photos are placed in front of the desk that used to be full of product documents. In the past, the cafe was bustling at this time, but now the people walking in and out are deserted. There is an eerie vibe in the air.

Your boss suddenly appeared by your seat, for you were shocked when you just came back to work after the holiday. You were still wondering why these white flowers, black and white photos, and the priest appeared in the company office? He read your signal from your wide eyes, then said seriously to you that the terrorist attacks took place on the top tourist resort in South Asia, where the Italian female colleague in the next office was unfortunately killed in the attacks.

As an upright man, your boss has military experience and is outraged by the ugly, indiscriminate killing of innocents by terrorists. Seeing your brows were furrowed, he patted you on the shoulder and promised that if one day you may meet thugs, he would pick up the gun and stand in front of you.

Rainbow Four: (6) Tempting Aroma

After completing the business trip, you pull the convenient suitcase from the airport to the taxi crossing. In winter at this time, you can still see bright flowers blooming arbitrarily on the branches, each exuding a tempting aroma like a censer, dancing and flying with the lazy evening breeze.

The radio in the taxi is playing brisk and soft classic songs, and the host's gentle voice just heals the busy crowd. The bright fire clouds rolled from the horizon are the raging flames released by the sun before it sinks into the sea. Some are like fluttering butterflies, and some are like fishes playing in the water.

As the company annual party is approaching, working in an international enterprise seems to be a common occurrence to celebrate popular festivals of different ethnic groups every now and then. The front foot just passed the Catholic Halloween, and the hind foot stepped into the Christian Christmas.

Your heart is a colorless stone, the scorching heat of the hot summer leaves no trace, and the falling snow of frosty winter is nowhere to be seen. It is difficult for you to enjoy the carnival-style grand feast as well as other colleagues, so you instinctively pursue where there are familiar figures and move closer. You are like a stray cat with a peculiar character, lying in a secluded place where no one is paying attention, meditating with your eyes open and closed.

The deep and distant night sky gave birth to the brilliance of the stars, and the majestic fashionable buildings lit up with bright lights. All employees of the Group's branches from all over the world, flying across the Strait of Malacca, over the Caribbean Islands, over the Mediterranean Sea, over the

Aegean Gulf, gathered together to celebrate the annual feast. Your boss and the top executives of the headquarters sat at the center round table at the front, with luminous cups of wine and food, singing and dancing to add the fun. Unexpectedly, the high-level representatives of the headquarters and your boss came to your table and shook hands with everyone.

At the peep of dawn, the thinking lark awakes in the morning light, where the whispers of all things come alive in the dream. The alarm clock rang, leaving last night's annual party to the moonlight. You climbed out of the soft satin blanket, walked into the steamy bathroom, cleaned yourself up, and welcomed the start of a new day.

Rainbow Four: (7) Spring after Spring

You are like a screw, diligently doing the work of sparing no effort. A multinational Group with huge body has its own solid management hierarchy. The managers at the top of the pyramid must be Europeans and Americans, the next may be Singaporeans and Hongkongers, then finally the mainlanders.

As a striving challenger, the ambition by passing the performance appraisal to get a job promotion, is not feasible in such a welfare-oriented European company. Everything has new arrivals, but the senior management team has not vacated the space, how is it possible to have a chance to climb up? Moreover, even if there is a change in the management, it is almost impossible for the mainlanders to fight for it, since the headquarters would continue arranging new Europeans and Americans to come in according to the rules.

After lunch, you occasionally look up at the sky, struggling with the gray reality of exhaustion and powerlessness. In the blink of an eye, you have worked hard to make a living in this company for many years. There is a saying that marriage has a seven-year itch, while the workplace may also have a similar wording. You are not ready for a life of marriage and children, you still have expanded skills for you to make more challenging choices, and most importantly, you still have the momentum to withstand the toss.

You are highly grateful to your boss for the careful cultivation of you along the way, so that you have the opportunity to reinvent yourself at work and thrive as a warrior who can fight alone, for he also knows that his position in the Asia-Pacific region will not last too long. When you send the thank-you letter from the company mailbox, the colleagues who get along well on weekdays feel regretful and feel that your resignation is like giving up the long-term meal ticket.

You are very motivated in your new career. One day, you received a call from your boss and asked if you were free to have a meal together. As a veritable foodie, of course you would take this opportunity to enjoy the high-end food. In the elegant and chic restaurant, he handed you a heavy purse to express his support for your new career. You said what to do if you couldn't pay it back, but he replied with a smile: it's okay; it can be repaid by the rest of your life.

Spring after spring, the earth reappears with new vitality. A swan as white as jade flew up from the picturesque lake, bringing you good news from afar. Fly a plane and practice gun shooting, your boss's life in Western Europe. You sniff your nose and admire him, then keep your head down and busy.

Rainbow Five: (1) A Drop of Sighing Dew

The time has changed, the sea and sky have changed, the mountains and rivers have changed, the cities and dreams have changed, but the melancholy has not changed.

The sandy beaches of the East Pacific coast, the vast international airports, everything ends up being irrelevant to you, and your dull memories are heavier than the cluttered, superfluous boulders. Sitting absent-mindedly in the long, narrow and empty chair, with eyes open to watch the endless stream of tourists, you see them as the unpredictable improvised shows, rushing to the end of their journey in the loud broadcast sound.

Not far from the front of the oblique side, there is an open beer bar. The exaggerated decoration style attracts many tourists to come here. You who don't drink alcohol and smoke a cigarette can't understand and feel the same. Why? They'd rather spend their time chasing for short-lived beer crazes.

The world outside the airport is cold and windy, while all living beings in the airport are running around. You will meet the tail of late autumn, like a drop of sighing dew rolling into a cold crystal cup. The lingering anguish in your heart blows you into that isolated attic, the sound of the mundanity is tapping your past memories, and the corners of your mind are scattered into black and white films. You put on a protective layer formed by perseverance, dive into the fluctuant night, light an ever-bright lantern that grows in the palm of your hand, and walk on the road from the vast river.

Two neat illustrated books are placed next to the coat in front of you. You don't intend to read them, but the process of waiting for the flight to take off is too long. The famous work of the world-renowned Nobel Prize in Literature is a gift from the person who is destined to you.Thinking of his cute and amiable image who looks like a national treasure panda, your dull journey will be painted with a bright color.

The stories in the books are the wise stars who are still awake from their dreams. The moonlight is so soft and calm, the sea wind has blown through the realm of ten thousand times, the ship of life inhabits a silent oasis, and the ghostly demon falls asleep soundly in the embrace of heaven and earth. You carefully open the window facing to a new world, as well as pick up the pen, ink and paper to write down your own poems and novels, where there are rivers, lakes and seas, and there are also thousands of lights.

Rainbow Five: (2) The Exotic Time

This is the place where your life takes a new direction. With the short black hair fluttering in the wind, you catch a glimpse of the increasingly visible white hair.

Returning to the exotic time of campus, feeling the vigor spirit of youth, you find the ancient international institution is immersed in a special learning atmosphere. You shuttle in different styles of teaching buildings, listen to professors explain the knowledge and common sense of different topics, and carve the future contour through the guides of predecessors.

Under the warm sunlight, the shadow of the ivory tower slipped quietly over the sunflower in front, and its forehead touched the fountain with a beautiful spinning figure. At this time, a fire of hope is ignited in your heart. You stand on tiptoe on the steps, with the eagerness in your eyes crossing the intertwined crowds in all directions, to chase the appearance of the destined person. You think that he looks very much like a panda, so he should be easy to identify.

You heard the sound of a broad leaf dancing, and you found the smell of flowers came from afar. He took off his suit and wore natural and decent casual clothes. He held a carefully prepared bouquet of red roses in his hand, after seeing you, slightly shy to give it to you solemnly. The smile like a flower bloomed on your long-lost face, as if returning to the eighteen-year-old age, and you thanked him gratefully.

From then on, a show of one person has become a choir of two. On the white paper you practice, on the book chapters you read, on the beach you walk along, and on the blue sky you see, silently you write down your and his names. He brings you familiar with every inch of the land here. A small grass to be unearthed, rings the doorbell of the soil, as she will witness the gentleness of the rain and the laughter of the sun together with the big tree next to her.

After watching the fantastic book fair, the two of you went to see the imaginative gallery side by side. The wind in the forest, swaying the flowers and trees on the alongside of the stone path, is it trying to tell you something privately? The sprites in the jungle whispered happily, jumping over the fingertips of the wind, going beyond the fence of the rain. Their happiness fell on the clean waves of the stream, on the heart of the strawberry, on the ear of the jade rabbit, and please you ran over to catch it.

Rainbow Five: (3) Take Root

This is the country known for its freedom and democracy. Different ethnicities from all over the world have crossed the oceans to reach this continent and take root here.

What is freedom and democracy? Is it really like its broadcast on TV? Is it really as described in the newspapers? Hot news confuses true and false, Internet celebrities distort right and wrong, multimedia creates social divisions, and big politicians promote racial discrimination. The fake contents are around daily life, yet you actually live in the information cocoon constructed by the Internet giants. Rational thinking is unknowingly corroded and submerged.

You are difficult to know who is right and who is wrong, then seeing is believing. You use your own weak and limited eyes to measure this country of freedom and democracy. You see it here, that the rich live unrestrainedly, with the luxurious castle villas, the extremely magnificent yachts, the limited-edition cars, the extravagant and wasteful delicacies, and the toxic lifestyles. Even if they violate the law, there is a dedicated team of accountants and lawyers to serve them. It is no wonder that the work related to finances and laws is so sought after, making it an accomplice to assist offenders in escaping crimes.

You see it here too, that the homeless are everywhere, near both sides of the shabby highway, at the piles of scrapped vehicles under the overpasses, in the messy corners of the busy street and alley, on the public area of the residential community, etc. Their humble tents are deeply needled in your hearts. Those who can't even afford a tent are unkempt and sleep on a dilapidated bench exposed to the sun and rain.

The capability of an ordinary person is very limited, without the active participation of local organizations and government institutions. By the growing disparity between the rich and the poor, the growing number of homeless will become larger and larger, while the various contradictions and problems will become more and more difficult to resolve. In the daily intercourse, the two of you are being more familiar with each other. You can see him helping some homeless from time to time, often giving cash, food, and necessities.

He always tells you that living in such a country, you must know how to protect yourself. The urban area where he lives belongs to the nice place gathering with higher education elites and talents, and the public security is in good condition. However, in urban areas that are generally predominantly Latino or African, you already know the dangers there.

Rainbow Five: (4) The Hazy Dusk

Lazy on weekends, you are tinkering with Chinese food in the kitchen in the morning which is another failed lesson. Why do Cantonese restaurants have dishes with an intoxicating aroma? While you cook according to the recipe, you make out horrible dishes with no taste but unbearable smell. You suddenly understand why did he joke that you don't have the talent to become a good chef.

After eating and drinking at noon, you sit in the co-pilot seat and watch him comfortably control the steering wheel. The original plan was to go on a road trip together by two cars, but he didn't expect your driving skills were so poor that you would have scratched the car before leaving the garage. He is fortunate that he has insurance reimbursement, and he shouldn't expect too much from you, a horrible new driver who got the driver license after failed many times.

Following the famous state road along the coastline, you are greeted with breathtaking natural landscapes. Vibrant cacti take root in the deep soil of the desert, and the afternoon sun slowly descends westward, coating the rocky granite with golden light. The vast land is connected to the boundless ocean, stretching to the distant sky. The waves nearby are flickering, the wings of gulls are silent in the sky, and the church bells are floating in prayer.

The air flow carrying the salty taste of the sea meets the dry wind pressure of the desert under the blue sky. The hazy dusk is approaching a little bit, where you seem to hear the whispers of lives hiding in the jungle pavilion, the mystery of the night wrinkling the dark ripples from the sea level.

You look at the persons in front, the objects in front, and the scenes in front, accidentally lost in contemplation. People's fictional god, when facing the chaos and orders of creation and destruction, facing the poor and weak souls in desperation, whether is he listening to their calls for help?

The day ends, the night gets darker, and the noise in your ears drifts away. You close the sleeping eyes and enter the dream of the galaxy. The soft morning light leaped over the end of the night, lit from the horizon of the sea and the sky, and the footsteps of the hour hand ran one circle after another. He takes you into his hobbies, to the finely brewed wine estate to taste the mellowness in the glass, to the green golf lawn to experience the peace of mind.

Rainbow Five: (5) A White Season

Flying in a straight line from country to country, you pack your luggage and embark on a journey to the European continent. The destination is a neutral country known as the world garden, which belongs to the richest developed country in the current era. In spring March, it's usually a gentle breeze and drizzle, but there is a white season with snowflakes.

Stepping out the gate of the international airport, you can see at a glance that he has been waiting for you in a long time, and his bright smile has dispelled the chill of the gloomy weather. He helped you to put your luggage in the rear compartment then slowly drove out the terminal parking garage. Although it was daytime, the sky outside was still like at night, where there was a thick fog.

A great elegant house appeared in front of you, and its attached large garden was neatly trimmed. At this time, only cold-resistant flowers and trees decorated in the entire courtyard. His parents are very knowledgeable and gentle, they speak four languages, and they are curious about you from the far East. They held your hand and walked slowly into the spacious book and painting halls, showing you the Tao Te Ching collection and the Ink Wash paintings with keen interest.

From the chat with his parents, you realized that the author of the two famous illustrated books he gave you before is his great grandpa. During the conversation, you can feel that they pay much attention to the family reputation, and count the famous missionary, doctor, mathematician, and writer who were from their Family Album. Thinking about yourself again, you also engage in amateur writing, but you have a weak writing skill, a low latitude thought, and an ordinary name.

You pop up in mind that your surname came from a holy king of the dynasty thousands of years ago. There are also many famous literati and military generals recorded on the genealogy, but these have nothing to do with you. Not all Chinese surnames are related to kings and generals? The Chinese civilization has a long history, and it is still difficult to count how many dynasties it has undergone. The most important difference between you and him is that he can inherit a lot of assets from his family, but your family seems to have nothing to inherit. You heard that your great grandparents were born as landlords, but they were tied and roamed in the streets after property deprived in old time.

The weather is rarely sunny, and the bright sun shines on the snow of the treetops, revealing a crystal brilliance. The idle days are long. When he takes you to visit the family museum and castle, you listen to him and the people around conversing in German, pronouncing the words like a muffled drum.

Rainbow Five: (6) The Beautiful Rays

It's your turn to wait for him, in the city where you live. A giant airport in the shape of a large fabulous bird, its exit hall for international flights, is crowded with people. You fidget and look around, with the phone in your bag, then in your pocket, then in your hand, for fear of missing the pick-up.

Leisurely, he came to you with a big suitcase, really like a clumsy and lovely national treasure panda. You are full of joy, guiding him into the car, facing the colorful sun, heading in the direction of hope, and the hot air drifts with the busy rhythm of the city.

This city is a young metropolis with great high technologies, full of shiny high-rise buildings, endless streets extending in all directions, and spotless roads lined with flowers and trees in orderly layers. The lush leaves, with the cool breeze blowing from the sea, soothe the mood of the hurried strugglers. The blue sky and white clouds, the blooming flowers and green trees, and the artwork-like residential architectures form here to be a beautiful home.

Lead him to experience the bustling city scene, then you with him get on the high-speed train running all the way to your wishful birthplace. In the quiet and leisurely countryside, there are brand-new white houses located at the green mountains and clear waters; clean cement roads extend to the gates of each household. The beautifully contoured peaks and ridges, the flowing streams and springs, all are busy telling you about their encounters with the stone bridges and the delicate flowers.

The starry sky at night is particularly charming. The bright moonlight covers the field under the sky with a pure veil, and the lamplights sway in the evening wind. In the countryside faraway, there is the sound of the natural piano played by frogs; in the center of the nearby lotus pond, fishes dance with the wonderful song. Please don't be surprised by the birds flying outside the window, stopping in the thicket to comb their beautiful feathers, you gently close your eyelids, and look forward to the rooster voice at sunrise.

You are grateful that you came to the world from this vibrant land, drinking the sweet spring water in the forest, also being with the stars, moon and sun on the branches. You woke up from the morning light, dressed in new clothes with him, placed the exactly tribute gifts of flowers, candies, dishes and fruits on the granite stone platform of the temple, and raised the cup by both hands respectfully with the spilled wine floated. From the beautiful rays of the sun, you wish the gods of heaven and earth and the ancestors of your family trees to bless you and him all well in life.

Rainbow Five: (7) Draw a Dream

In the vast sea of people, you and him meet and know each other. This is a very rare destiny. Straighten your fingers and calculate that the golden autumn October is the right time to open the gate of marriage, where the splendid roses are richly fragrant, and the dew drops are brightly crystal. He will hold your hand and go to the future together.

The two of you hit it off and keep everything simple, saving the tedious and complicated wedding planning. Bring your both necessary documents, step into the inconspicuous Civil Affairs Bureau together, and carefully go through the process of the marriage registration. After taking the oath, you and him will hold the marriage certificate in hands, then will be called wife and husband in the future. The simple wedding rings on each other's fingers are like the red thread of marriage given by the heaven Matchmaker, one end is connected to you and the other end is connected to him.

Colored light shines into the secluded forest in your heart, the stilly lake is rippling with blue waves, as well as the brilliant rainbow glows across the sky. You used to think that you would gradually live to be an old aunt with a lonely life, the children of your cousins are about to grow up, while you would be no longer young. When you finally get married, let the worries that often surround your family members disappear into thin air. They wish you and him as wife and husband will stay long together and grow old together.

The living situation has not changed much after marriage, you and him are walking in the wind and the sun, as well as the occasional bickering is the spice of livelihood. In the journey of life where people come and go, you and him have both encountered joys and sorrows. Those ruthless and barren souls, are unable to blossom and grow into big trees.

Next to the holiday house, listening to the sea breeze blowing, watching the waves bloom, you draw a dream in the name as his wife. You and him meet in winter, reunite in summer. The seasons change, yet sincere greetings never go away. Spring and autumn are constantly flowing in the time, and he will wait for you in the future reincarnation.

Last night, you were laying in the colorful April sky, hearkening to butterflies say that the blooming buds nourished by morning dew are the most intoxicating; hearkening to bees say that the natural flower stamens can brew the sweetest honey; hearkening to ants say that the flowers and plants are nostalgic for the warmth of soil and raindrops. Today, you are yawning in the colorful River town, after reading a classic ancient book, and you start to dream with him for having adorable children.

Clovers
(1) You are just born

The rainy weather is still in middle January;
Southern China is now in the cold winter.
The ticking bell sounded at four on the afternoon;
Your father walked back and forth anxiously outside the
obstetrics of the city hospital.

With the crisp and joyful wow baby crying,
You have finally come in our long hope.
Dear little niece, you are welcome to join our world;
Become a new member of our family, and the beginning of a
new generation.

Your grandparents, my parents,
Dress up the baby room at home early;
Every day they think about the first grandkid arriving,
With your mother to wait for you nervously and happily.

I, who was newly married, live far away from you with eight
time zones;
Watch your first photo of your birth with your uncle.
Your little sleeping face has a sweet smile like that red apple;
I can't help sighing how amazing the life that was born in ten
months of the pregnancy.

(2) You are just one month old

Early in the morning, your mom sent me your photo with
interest.
Today you are wearing new clothes and new flowers to
celebrate the full month;
The chubby little hands wear the golden jade strings from your
grandparents,
Implied that the little baby, you can thrive healthily and
happily.

Your grandparents have already visited the fortune teller with
your birthday;
She gave you a very sweet name along your destiny astrology.
I hope that you, such as swallow bird, will have a happy and
meaningful life.

The overseas WeChat video pulls everyone close together.
I smiled and said: What? Give my niece such an ugly name?
My parents blamed me cheerfully for not being able to
appreciate it.
Brother and Sister-in-law smiled and hugged you gently,
patting you to sleep.

You have your first beloved toy, a cute baby elephant.
I heard that you are a natural small alarm clock that wakes up
at 6am every morning.
After drinking milk, as long as the baby elephant next to you,
you will immediately be well behaved.
Looking at your powerful black eyes and quiet little face,
I would think that this child may grow into a person with
positive energy and she is not fussy.

(3) You are two months old

A little later, you look more and more like your dad.
Hands and feet kept moving while sleeping, humming again
then fell asleep.

Due to your weak constitution, your stomach is bloated and
you has baby eczema.
My brother was so anxious that he took you to the hospital
overnight.
After several days of careful treatment and bathing with
Chinese herbs,
With the peeling skin removal like fish scales on the whole
body,
Little baby, you are finally back full of energy.

Your mom takes you to swim during the day, but it is just
bubble water.
No one thought you would fall asleep like a tittle lion when
arrived at the swimming pool.
No matter how loud the surrounding noise is, it can't interrupt
your sweet dreams.
At night you become a naughty little bad angel who keeps
wriggling;
You need to hear your parents sing nursery rhymes while they
are holding you.

You start to recognize people, stick to your mom all day,
And can't stop crying when your mom is during a bath;
Your dad sits on the side yet eats guavas to make you quiet.

Lying in the pink cradle, you open your innocent eyes then lick
your little finger;

Maybe it is fun, you take your little finger away then put it
back in your mouth again;
As if you are immersed in yourself beautiful hours: your
parents can't bear to bother you.

(4) You are three months old

You just have a new hairstyle, now more like a boy.
Sleeping postures are also becoming more casual:
From time to time, a difficult S-type,
Face-down frog-type,
Like a caterpillar with a small sheet.
You are always full of curiosity and love to stick your little
tongue out.

Recently you learned to look up and sideways.
Awake from a nap, you will try to get up and learn to turn over
on your own;
If you don't try it many times, you will get angry.
Your parents help you turn back and forth till tired;
Put you back to sleep or turn over by yourself.
But you can't turn over, you feel very frustrated to yourself.

You often make out babble voice as your own language;
You also know how to pick up your favorite little toy.
All the stuff on the toy bed is piled up next to you;
You are sleeping lazily aside the big pacifier with your half
closed eyes.
Sometimes you pretended to cry a few sounds to see how your
parents reacted.

On your own small bath tub, there were floating little yellow ducks and cups,
Then you took a vacation-like leisurely pose and giggled.
You put whatever you see in your mouth after shower: my little naughty girl.

(5) You are four months old

The greatest fun of your grandparents is to tease you every day;
A few words humming in their mouth: The granddaughter's temperament is very like her aunt.
Your grandparents bought new clothes then brought you to take too many sets of artistic photos;
They often happily showed your funny pictures and videos in the WeChat groups of friends and relatives.

You have learned to eat rice cereal, but you will spit it out when it is tasteless.
Later, your grandma put you on a big earthy red drool mask;
Also, she cleverly put fruit sweetness in the pacifier toy for you to bite.

The family made your cryings and laughings into an extremely vivid expression pack;
I heard that it is going to be a small surprise gift for you when you reach 18 years old.

Seeing you leap around in the crib and scratching toys,
As your aunt, I am in concern: "Oh, hello, you will break these poor pendant toys!"
It is estimated that your dad will have to work harder to earn money for buying you new toys and beds.

On the traditional festival day, the bright sun was shining
pleasantly outside.
Drag on the little bottle that is always with you, filled with cool
boiling water,
The family happily pushed you on the stroller to go shopping
and walk around the river.
Seeing passers-by coming, you greeted warmly with your
hands and feet.
When you get to the dinner table in the evening, you rush to
grab food eagerly, my little niece.

(6) You are five months old

An annual celebration was held in the swimming pool;
You and your mom won two cans of newly imported milk
powder.
When you see the delicious milk powder, you stare at it with
hungry eyes-look;
As long as you are at the swimming pool, you can't wait to
jump in the funny bubble water.

You followed your parents to visit the little elder cousin who
lived not far away.
Seeing the little elder cousin eating the corn by herself,
You pitifully stared at the corn while picking your feet.
Suddenly, you stretched out your two small hands to grab the
corn in crying;
The adults next to you looked at you like a cute little bad angel
and all laughed;
In the end, with the sharing from the little elder cousin, you
both became good friends.

After kindergarten, the little elder brothers from next doors
often came to see you.
Holding a bunch of toys together, they wanted to show you
how to play these toys.
Your mom sent me a few videos saying her daughter was
sitting totally like a boss;
With a bell toy in your hand, you looked at the little elder
brothers without blinking.
I joked: my young niece has a leadership style, and she will
grow up to be a big sister.

You are so excited that you can turn around arbitrarily.
Every night on the big toy bed, you roll back and forth from the
ends of the bed.
Sitting on the newly bought baby table-chair, you move with
great excitement.
Your grandparents love to act as the two funny bears from
cartoon series in front of you, amusing their granddaughter,
And you laugh out a few high tones.

(7) You are half year old

You can sit on the soft sofa a little bit by yourself;
When lying down, you take a plastic ball in your hands and
carry another one on your feet;
With the full attention, maybe you will be a good seed for
football in the future.
Your dad is used as a funny trojan chair, holding you around;
Makes you laugh loudly with your cute mouth open but no
small teeth growing yet.

When you see a box of milk placed on the table, you straighten
your small arms to take it;
It's surprised you learn that the soft straw is used for absorbing
milk in your little mouth.
Your mom had to pack up her cell phone and computer far
away from you,
Worrying that the little baby, you would wave your hands and
feet tirelessly to rush for play.

Your grandparents took back a blue carpet with full of marine
animals from a relative's house.
They said it is to cultivate a sense of environmental protection
for the granddaughter from early age.
You are so happy to climb on this recycled blue carpet,
Sometimes getting up and raising your little finger to scream
forward like a little bird,
Sometimes chasing the colorful plastic balls rolling beside,
Sometimes curiously staring at the marine animals on the
carpet seemed to count.

When the weather is nice, family will take you to the children's
playground in the community.
Listening to the beautiful and joyful children's songs, also
looking at all kinds of intellectual toys;
You are there for hours, and you meet many cute friends.
When family takes pictures for you with phone, you are riding
on a little sheep toy car with music;
It seems you know how to focus at once, staring at phone
sharply, and putting on a fixed pose.

(8) You are seven months old

You sit obediently in the lens of the phone,
Holding the little pink pacifier in hand and looking down
intently; what are you doing?
Ahahaha! You are so cute. It turns out you give the pacifier for
feeding your little feet.
At the same time, you raise your head as well as open your cute
little mouth to laugh happily.

In the evening, you almost take a half-hour bath by your
grandma in the bathroom.
After bathing, you are dressed in a nice floral skirt then put to
sit on a soft table-chair.
You grabbed a milk bottle that was even bigger than your face
and drank it with interest.
It is fun neither to cry nor to make trouble, that you winked like
a little grown-up in thought.

Whether you see your grandpa's blue porcelain tea cup or your
grandma's TV remote control;
Whether you see your dad's mobile phone or your mom's
computer on the table;
You always open a pair of curious eyes and stretch out a pair of
tender hands desperately trying to get it.
After you couldn't get it, you slyly knocked down the bottle on
the side to vent your inexplicable temper.

When you are excited, you will dance with your little palms to
pat your little feet, with your mouth humming;
There is a glittering bow-knot on your forehead, and there is a
bright baby smile on your face.
You look at yourself in the video, yet you are very playful,
funnily wanting to touch and kiss yourself.

During busy time, your mom will take you to her fashion
studio and place you in a rattan rocking chair;
Let you lie comfortably in the rocking chair, stretching your
little legs lazily and lightly with your little fingers.
When your mom is off work, she will take you to the big
supermarket nearby to buy baby products and meats;
You are also very excited sitting in the cart, sticking out your
little tongue and staring at the surrounding goods.

(9) You are eight months old

Family bought a new blue baby walker for you;
Sitting in this blue walker, you can go back and forth as long as
your feet are on the ground.
You are laughing and patting the table toys when the little
wheels move;
You are also curious to see your grandpa mopping the floor,
chasing him back and forward.

Your mom complained that her daughter might be violent to hit
the toys;
When I open the video, I sigh: This is not violent! My little
niece is clearly the excitement of the chick!
You wear glittering rabbit ears, put on flower shoes and follow
your parents to the square at night.
People around see you are cute and chubby sitting in the
stroller; they want to give you warm hugs.

Your grandparents say it's too hot and want to give the
granddaughter a refreshing new hairstyle.
Ahahaha! It turns out that the new hairstyle is just to give you a
shaved bald head!

After shaving, your grandparents put the little pig toys on the floor and let you chase the toys cheerfully.
The little elder brothers from next doors come to visit you, as well as play their electric guitars for you.

Due to the changeable weather, you catch a cold and fever accompanied by inflammation.
As a baby, your throat and stomach are uncomfortable; you vomit whatever you drink or eat.
Looking at you who are noisy and tired, there are many red dots on your face and body too;
The whole family is very distressed, bringing you rush to the hospital for a few injections.
After several days, you slowly get improved and recover, then my anxiety also calmed down.

(10) You are nine months old

It is time to quit human milk, even though you are not quite used to the taste of rice cereal;
After waking up at noon, you crawl around like a little lion to find your milk bottle.
Your parents tease that, their daughter is getting lazy who doesn't even want to hold a bottle;
Just put the milk bottle on the carpet then drink quietly in a squatting posture.
When you see the sliced apples, you catch them to your mouth regardless of having no teeth yet.

After dinner, you are naughty around to let family bring you to see the bustling night scene;

If they don't take you out, you will pretend cry with the tearful innocent eyes but look cute.
Every day after 9pm, you will be able to fall asleep in the crib and seldom get bothering;
Your parents sometimes put you in a kitten sleeping bag then take funny pictures or videos of you.

My little niece, you seem to have a smiling face like a little joyful Buddha;
Neighborhood's grandpas and grandmas in the nearby garden also like you;
Whenever they see you out to play, they will casually come over to kindly tease you.

In the spare time, your mom takes out your clothes from the full month and puts them on you again,
Finding that you are quite happy with the old clothes, especially the little red hooded fox.
You also seem to know how to shake your hands and hold your parents' phones to take pictures for yourself.
When you see a trash can in the shape of a yellow duck next to your parents, you are distracted;
You make the little feet quietly kick it and squint from time to time to see whether your parents catch you.

(11) You are ten months old

The weather is very sunny, and the whole family go for a walk
in the East Mountain Park.
Your grandpa insisted on holding you up to over two hundred
stone steps, tired with bending back;
Ahahaha! He can't stand it then wanted to put you back in your
dad's arm.
East Mountain Park is an old attraction of the city, built on the
top of a high mountain;
I often climbed the mountain alone when I was in middle
school, especially at the rebellious age.

You enjoy to stay in the playground of the community;
Either lie on the stone table or always want to try on the
children's slide.
Seeing a lot of little brothers and sisters playing around,
You dance with joy, also try to climb over, and play with them
together.

Your parents are happy to take you to visit their friends nearby.
Three children included you are sitting on the rug, with various
intellectual toys piled around.
You stare at the snack on the side of the little boy who is
similar age to you;
When he is paying attention to watching the cartoon movie,
you try to grab his snack;
However, you can't make it success, then you know how to pull
the elder sister with your finger to help you.

Your grandma folded a big flower with the pretty turban and
carried it on your little round head;
You are cheerful for going to the neighbor's house to play with
the little elder brothers and show them the flower on head.

While the little elder brothers are age in primary school, act
like little adults no longer playing around as they used to;
Their dad put you on the little elder brothers' desk, yet you grab
their pens and books curiously;
The little elder brothers are so anxious that they sweat coldly,
for fearing you would throw away their treasured things.

(12) You are eleven months old

For celebrating your grandpa's 60th birthday, my husband and I
flew back to China;
The long flight journey about 12 hours was indeed a bit dull.
I watched intently your photos and videos on my tablet;
My husband joked to me with a slight jealousy that I care you
more than I caring him .

In the south of China, even in the winter, the climate is still
pleasant, neither cold nor hot;
Unlike Europe at this time, it is always shrouded in the gloomy
and cold weather.
As soon as we got off the plane and waited for the baggage,
your grandparents called us eagerly;
You saw your grandparents talking on the phone and wanted to
grab it with humming voice;
I was making fun of my parents on the phone: What? Your
granddaughter is too young to speak yet~

Around an hour of high-speed train, we came to the city where
I was born, also where you were born.
The whole family happily greeted us into the house, while you
seemed to be a little afraid of us as strangers;

Obediently crawling in the arms of your parents, small round
eyes peeking at us from time to time.
Your grandma said that you usually are very active: how can
you be so shy when see your aunt and uncle?
When your mother was pregnant with you, I was just married
to abroad. This is our first meeting.

Relatives also came in the evening for dinner and congratulated
your grandpa on his 60-year-old birthday.
Those little cousins love to run around you, pinching gently
your chubby face from time to time;
While you sit on the children's chair quietly, staring at me and
your uncle curiously.
Are you thinking why does your uncle look different from
everyone? Where does your aunt come from?
Your grandfather said happily that he is satisfied with children
married and grandchildren well healthy!

(13) You are one year old

You have teeth in your jaw now, white and pointed, like tiny
tiger teeth.
Your dad took you to the restaurant, yet you learned by
yourself to grab the food naturally.
Your mom said that you would make a cry, when you saw all
family eating at table without you.
Give you a bowl with a few meats and vegetable, and you
know how to eat quietly by bowing your head.

Your grandmother's family entered a new house in the outer
city, and your grandparents are invited;

Little one, you also know how to pull your grandparents'
trousers to ask them bring you;
No matter how your parents to pet you, you still want to chase
your grandparents with the little short legs.

The toy baby elephant accompanied you since you were full
month becomes your good companion;
Now you not only stand up and crawl on your own, but you
also are a toddler.
You like to crawl around on the bed for a while, then hold the
baby elephant for a while and talk;
Your play the baby elephant's long nose, touch her big ear, as
well as kiss her mouth.

Your dad is a big lazy man, and he often eats delicious fruit or
meat on the sofa;
But he forgets there is a baby girl, his beloved little daughter
who is pitifully drooling;
Your mom couldn't stand it then scold your dad in smile, also
pretending to kick her husband away.
I feel that the more you grow, the more you will look like your
dad to see food as the favorite.

At your birthday party, the relatives drive to arrive early for
seeing you,
Bringing you beautiful gifts and exquisite cakes to make you
laugh happily.
Your grandparents cook you the birthday eggs and painted
them with cute and well wishes.
From afar, I sincerely hope my dear little niece to grow up
healthily and move forward bravely!

Lotus Romance
Chapter 1: First Meet

The young boy of Lingshan Academy, Mu Yunchen, went out with his uncle Mu Fuzi just after he was ten years old.

Walking along the mountains and rivers, they forgot the distance of the road. When Mu Yunchen with his uncle Mu Fuzi arrived at an unknown and beautiful island, they entered along the gurgling stream, where the grasses are secluded, the flowers are fragrant and the butterflies are colorful. With the melodious sound of birdsong, a glazed courtyard appeared beside the lotus lake. Mu Yunchen slowly approached the yard, but in the chic and fragrant main hall, he was delighted to see the newly born baby girl sleeping in a handful of half-opened and half-closed lotus petals and leaves.

Mu Yunchen hurriedly came to inform his uncle and invited him to explore along with him. After careful inspection, he found that the lotus holding the baby girl was surrounded by layers of glittering gold, and even his uncle Mu Fuzi could not touch it. Mu Yunchen looked at the sleeping baby girl with soft eyes, and tried to touch it gently with his fingers. When the fingertips felt it, the layers of golden light immediately gathered into the words: My wife and I meet the time limit; My baby will wait for her destined man to come here (Baby: Hua Qianyu).

As the words faded away, the baby girl in the petals seemed to wake up from a dream, staring at Mu Yunchen with small round eyes, as clear as elves. Uncle Mu Fuzi said meaningfully to Mu Yunchen by the side: "Presumably this place should be a quiet place for immortals outside the world, and those who are

not of extremely high character should not be approached. You
are destined for this baby."

Then the uncle carefully picked up the lively baby girl with
little fingers, the lying lotus leaves and petals instantly turned
into a teardrop crystal shining with golden light and
disappeared into the baby girl's heart. Mu Yunchen and his
uncle stopped for a while and took the baby girl out of the lotus
lake. The scene behind them was also instantly hidden in the
clouds of the island.

Chapter 2: Growing up

After returning to Lingshan Academy, in order to avoid
everyone's unpredictable words and deeds, Uncle Mu Fuzi only
let the cronies know that the young boy Mu Yunchen's first
travels found an orphaned baby named with Hua Qianyu. He
quietly placed her in the distant and quiet Qingxin Pavilion,
and gave her to the Nanny to raise her carefully.

Lingshan, this is a rare fairyland in the world, with numerous
peaks, misty clouds, surrounded by streams, and flying
waterfalls. The central academy founded by the ancestor of
Xianmen is located on the majestic main peak. While the
Qingxin Pavilion is located in a remote mountain peak. It was
built by Mu Yunchen's parents in the early years. Usually, few
people visit it. Only Mu Yunchen occasionally visits and sleeps
on the couch for a while.

Mu Yunchen's parents were the heads of Lingshan Academy,
but unfortunately they both died unexpectedly when they were
young. His uncle, Mu Fuzi, has no intention of getting married
all his life. He has been focusing on taking care of the affairs of

Lingshan Academy all the year round, regards Mu Yunchen as his own, and strictly teaches him everything. The arrival of the baby girl Hua Qianyu seems to open up a hazy world for Mu Yunchen at this time: with each other, the loneliness is no longer there.

The days pass by the thousands of green branches and flowers with the breeze, and Hua Qianyu of Qingxin Pavilion is no longer a swaddled baby waiting to be fed. When she was one year old, she would laugh and walk as a toddler; when she was two years old, she would stand among the flowers and run after colorful butterflies; when she was three years old, she would stand on her short legs and raise her hands to ask Mu Yunchen for a hug; when she was four years old, she would sit down obediently next to Uncle Mu Fuzi and gulp and eat the peach. When Hua Qianyu was five years old, it happened to be the fifteen years old of Mu Yunchen. After the ceremony of binding his hair, Mu Yunchen had to do the seclusion practice, focusing on his improvement. Hua Qianyu was also often alone and began to learn.

The lush years are like the passing water. Although Mu Yunchen was young when he completed the seclusion practice, he was already with the immortal energy. He was tall and attractive, with his temperament naturally elegant and deserted. He was dressed in elegant white clothes which made him look extremely handsome.

Chapter 3: Seeking Knowledge

In the blink of an eye, Hua Qianyu has reached the cardamom age, with thick hair hanging down to her shoulders, slim, graceful and beautiful, with a powerful aura.

Mu Yunchen has become more and more exquisite in his practice since the royal crown age. After many examinations, he officially took over the position as the Head of Lingshan Academy, and followed the sayings: "Be in your position; Think about your responsibility." Busy with all the important things. Uncle Mu Fuzi devoted himself to teaching. Hua Qianyu is talented and intelligent. After quickly completing the assigned academic affairs, she is often alone, occasionally hiding in the distance and watching Mu Yunchen busy, or curiously overhearing Uncle Mu Fuzi's lectures.

Lingshan Academy has a long-standing reputation and a wealth of talents. It has always been famous with teachers and apprentices. There are vast numbers of famous and aristocratic families vying to visit, and those who can come to Lingshan Academy to study should be the best among the families. Hua Qianyu loves learning and realizes: "Reading books can make me wise, studying arts can make me feel sensible, practicing hard skills can defend myself, and seeking medical treatments can heal people." She is interested in everything. Mu Yunchen thought about Hua Qianyu's thirst for knowledge, so he discussed with his uncle and put Hua Qianyu in the academy, becoming the youngest student in the class.

Because of being alone all the year round, Hua Qianyu is not used to talking with people, and whenever someone approaches inexplicably, she consciously keeps a distance. She was only acquainted with Wei Youli and Mo Xuanxi at the nearby tables.

Although Mo Xuanxi is a girl, she is handsome and valiant. It is said that her parents have no boys, and they are not afraid of conventions, raising their three daughters as boys since childhood. But Wei Youli is a boy, however, he looks more delicate than a girl. He is a lovable young master who always enjoys talking, the youngest in the family is loved by his parents, and two elder sisters are married.

Although Hua Qianyu has been keeping a low profile since she entered the academy, sitting quietly in a corner, it is still picturesque, still attracting the attention of all the students, marveling at her pure appearance and temperament that they have never been seen before. On the other hand, Jiang Zilan, who was in the front row of the academy, didn't like Hua Qianyu much.

Jiang Zilan is arrogant and charming, comes from the family of the richest man in Xianmen, and is the only daughter of her parents. Relying on the infinite doting of the family, she is arrogant and domineering. In the Family Chat, she encounters Mu Yunchen by chance. She is stunned that there is such a perfect person in the world, and she is obsessed with him, planning to marry Mu Yunchen one day. Therefore, coming to Lingshan to study is also intentionally close to Mu Yunchen.

Chapter 4: Out of Mountain

After the years of study, Hua Qianyu is just over the hairpin age. Uncle Mu Fuzi invited her to the front hall of the main peak, and asked her to make a wish. Hua Qianyu replied: "According to the right way, live up to the heart, follow the rule, and attach great importance to teaching, for the public and selfless." Uncle Mu Fuzi said with joy on his face: "Yunchen has been granted the sacred wooden whip, and you with Yunchen have the same aspirations." After speaking, he happily gave the sacred flower whip to Hua Qianyu, and asked her to go out with Mu Yunchen to deal with the chaos.

The sacred flower whip in the hand of Hua Qianyu can turn into blossoming petals, and with the dance-like movements, it can hurt or save people. While Mu Yunchen's sacred wooden whip can be turned into leaves, and with the stirring notes, it can awaken or sway the mind, killing enemies invisibly.

Hua Qianyu was dressed in simple green clothes, like a hibiscus emerging from the water, standing two steps away from Mu Yunchen, a little shy and uneasy. Mu Yunchen stared at Hua Qianyu with soft light in his eyes. He recalled that although he first met her when he was a child, they seldom got along, but he never forgot his concern. He stepped forward and said with a smile: "Qianyu, don't be afraid of me."

After a while to change into light clothes, the two opened the barrier and left Lingshan. When they descended to the plain, they saw the sky was clear, the air was fresh, and a flock of birds were flying. They kept going forward. It is the river and sea ahead. The islands are scattered on the wave surface like stars. The blue water beats on the beach rocks, stirring up layers of waves, like pearls floating in rows. Listening carefully, it seems can hear countless waves from the sky with the continuous moving whispers or the melodious songs sung by the beautiful Mermaid Diva for the guests. Hua Qianyu took a deep breath, the clear air flowing into her nose, touching the heartstrings, as if on the verge of a colorful dream, she felt happy and refreshed. Hua Qianyu couldn't help but whisper: "It's so beautiful…" Mu Yunchen saw her movings and her brows, and his eyes were as gentle as honey.

Not long after, the two rushed to the place where the chaos happened, and it turned out that Chi Yanyan, the son of the current Immortal Governor, was making trouble here. This person is not only ruthless, but also lustful and has many wives and concubines. Seeing the beautiful wife of the Suzerain Master of the Sang family, he sent strong troops to rob the territory and her. Fortunately, Mu Yunchen and Hua Qianyu stopped them in time, then Chi Yanyan hated Mu Yunchen even more and coveted Hua Qianyu. He said in vicious words: "Hua Qianyu? It's more in line with me." Aroused the outrage, Mu Yunchen immediately protected Hua Qianyu behind him, angrily looking down at Chi Yanyan fleeing.

After dealing with the troubles in this area, the Suzerain Master Sang gratefully invited the two of them to take a seat. Mu Yunchen talked for a while, thanked the Suzerain Master Sang for his warm hospitality, and motioned Hua Qianyu to leave together.

Before returning, Mu Yunchen planned to take Hua Qianyu to see the mortal world outside Lingshan. After getting along for some time, Hua Qianyu gradually became familiar with Mu Yunchen and used to having him beside her, which seemed to be an innate tacit understanding. The two came to the most prosperous town in the mortal world, which coincided with the local Lantern Festival, very lively and dizzying. The appearance of Mu Yunchen and Hua Qianyu side by side caused quite a commotion in the crowded streets. Every mortal admired them as an immortal couple and gave them auspicious lamps and poems.

They stepped into the elegantly decorated hotel, where the proprietress arranged a one-room suite for them, knowing whether it was intentional or not, claiming that there were no vacant hotels within ten miles because of the festival. Hua Qianyu didn't mind, as Mu Yunchen gave her an inexplicable peace of mind, and soon fell asleep. Mu Yunchen sat lightly on the bedside, looked at Hua Qianyu's baby-like sleeping position, and reached out his hand to caress her cheek softly. After Hua Qianyu felt the warm touch, she couldn't help rubbing Mu Yunchen's palm. At this time, the night of the Lantern Festival is fascinating.

Chapter 5: Travel with Friends

There is not much peaceful nowadays. The current Immortal Governor in power is brutal and arbitrary, arrogant and lawless, causing constant scourges in the world, and the people are displaced. Hua Qianyu followed Mu Yunchen out of the mountains to quell the chaos many times. Her cultivation improved rapidly, and her mana was so pure that she was already able to stand on her own. Uncle Mu Fuzi thinks that Mu Yunchen doesn't need to worry about Hua Qianyu going out to the mountains alone.

Hua Qianyu's friends Wei Youli and Mo Xuanxi send messages to sincerely invite Hua Qianyu to visit them and travel together before returning to Lingshan. Hua Qianyu decided to go to the Wei family first and then go to the Mo family. As soon as she stepped into the gate, Wei Youli's cheerful voice came: "Sister Qianyu, I've been waiting for you!" After saying goodbye to his parents in a hurry, he couldn't wait to rush to the Mo family with Hua Qianyu.

Mo Xuanxi's elder twin sisters, who just got married not long ago, recruited two good husbands, and the family was happy. When the Mo family saw Hua Qianyu, they thought in a trance that she was an elf fairy who strayed into the mortal world, and they couldn't put it down with joy. They insisted on warmly entertaining Hua Qianyu and Wei Youli for a few more days before letting their youngest daughter set out on a tour with them.

The three accompanied all the way to a beautiful place, but found that the people there, men, women and children, looked confused and dumb as puppets. Hua Qianyu wanted to find out what happened. The three stayed there for many days, and finally found a wise man in his twilight years to tell the reason: "This place is originally beautiful, with outstanding people, but the current Immortal Governor many years ago suddenly broke in. He grabbed the spirit stone hidden in the spring, and since then destroyed the Feng Shui of this place. Over time, the people living here will become demented and short-lived. The world is so dark!" Hua Qianyu flew to look at the spring and found that there was a way to save it. So she took out the sacred flower whip and from it transformed into a longevity flower, sorted out a ray of spiritual energy from her body and placed it in the spring to the left and right, then the Feng Shui there was finally reborn. The old wise man and the people were very grateful to Hua Qianyu, and they lined up in a long line to see off the three of them.

Chapter 6: Suzerain Disaster

The newborn calves are not afraid of tigers, so the three of them plan to secretly find out the devil-headed Immortal Governor manipulating the spirit stone for what purpose.

Before ready to go, Wei Youli suddenly encountered an urgent report from his family. The commander of the Immortal

Governor led a large group of troops to attack the Wei family's territory, burn, kill and plunder, and the situation was at stake. When the three of them rushed to the Wei's house in a hurry, the old Suzerain Master Wei and his old lady were doing their best to resist, however the entire land was destroyed beyond its original appearance. Hua Qianyu asked Wei Youli and Mo Xuanxi to help the seriously injured people to a safe place to settle down. She swept the enemy with her sacred flower whip, which was an artifact worth thousands of weapons, beat the opponents to pieces, and protected the lifeblood and boundary of the Wei family for not being destroyed by the main force sent by the Immortal Governor.

Hua Qianyu has the ability to heal people. She was bound to treat the wounded of the Wei family. When Wei Youli saw that his parents had been saved by Hua Qianyu, he hugged Hua Qianyu with tears in his eyes and cried like a very injured child. The killing scene was terrifying. Hua Qianyu prepared to rest behind the closed door for the whole day and wait for the mana to recover before saying goodbye. But she never thought that she would receive a message early in the morning that the Mo family, which is thousands of miles away, was also attacked from a large group of troops led by another commander of the Immortal Governor. Hua Qianyu took out two golden lotus petals from her body and handed them over to Wei Youli: "This petal can generate a magical barrier to help you avoid damage in the realm." After speaking, Hua Qianyu and Mo Xuanxi rushed to rescue the Mo family. Wei Youli gave the two golden lotus petals to his parents, and the three of them bowed to the two elders then left together.

When they arrived at the Mo family boundary, most of the buildings had been destroyed by the invaders, as well as the clans were killed and injured countless times. Wei Youli and

Mo Xuanxi joined the sturdy Mo family to fight bravely against the enemy. In Hua Qianyu's hands, thousands of tiny petals with tiny stars flew like sharp arrows to the invading Immortal Governor's troops, defeating them one after another, and finally ensuring the peace for the Mo family.

Chapter 7: Imprisonment

Hua Qianyu felt that it was horrific conspiracy for the Immortal Governor to send troops to persecute famous and aristocratic families in various suzerains.

After the Mo family was settled, the old Suzerain Master Mo and his old lady asked their youngest daughter, Mo Xuanxi, the women's hero, to assist Wei Youli to return to the Wei family's territory to help the Wei family rebuild their home. Then Hua Qianyu said goodbye to them who were reluctant to part, and prepared to set off back to Lingshan.

The Immortal Governor's son, Chi Yanyan, led the masters waiting on Hua Qianyu's way back to Lingshan. Since Hua Qianyu spent too much energy in this trip to quell the chaos, she couldn't completely defeat the aggressive masters. Before being arrested, she secretly sent a signal to Mu Yunchen, who was far away in Lingshan, and was forcibly taken away by Chi Yanyan with others.

Chi Yanyan placed Hua Qianyu in the Governor's Palace. But he couldn't get close to her, even the masters had no ideas. Only after Hua Qianyu was brought to the Immortal Governor's secret place, she pretended to be unconscious, however accidentally caught sight of the Immortal Governor using the spirit stone to absorb and control the densely packed puppet army, and couldn't help feeling apprehensions. The Immortal Governor saw that Hua Qianyu was a rare genius, then he intended to make her a top-level puppet, but Chi Yanyan refused by all means. How could the stunning beauty whom he was about to get would be wasted into a puppet! "Father, leave her to me." The Immortal Governor couldn't stand his beloved son too obsessed with this young woman's beauty, so he changed his mind. As for why Chi Yanyan couldn't get close to Hua Qianyu, the Immortal Governor thought that this young woman was protected by the special aura. Put her in the Monster Cave for some time, and let the Monster sealed for hundreds of years absorb her aura.

Chi Yanyan figured that there was no other more efficient way, But he imagined as soon as Hua Qianyu would be removed from the forbidden body by the Monster in a few days, he could completely possess her from then on, and he was extremely lustful, which made him become over exultation. He personally followed the Immortal Governor's subordinates and saw Hua Qianyu lying in the Monster Cave like a sleeping fairy, so he touched the coveted saliva and left.

Chapter 8: Rescue

When Mu Yunchen received the signal from Hua Qianyu, he couldn't help but panic, then went to the front hall of the main peak of Lingshan Academy to inform his uncle Mu Fuzi. There were also bursts of worry from his uncle, and Mu Yunchen flew to the Immortal Governor's land involuntarily.

The Immortal Governor's land is heavily guarded everywhere, full of the devil atmosphere of bullying. After a lot of quiet inquiries, Mu Yunchen learned that Hua Qianyu was placed under house arrest in the Monster Cave. After some time, the Monster sucked Hua Qianyu's spiritual energy away, making her lose all the mana, then the Immortal Governor's son Chi Yanyan would bring her into his Mansion and forcibly occupy her. Mu Yunchen let the rustling evening wind blow his bright hair with a jade crown, and his long white clothes fluttered along with it. The cold and handsome face could hardly detect the anger in his heart, but his deep eyes swept across a glimpse of harshness. In order not to act rashly and alert the enemy, Mu Yunchen sneaked into the Monster Cave.

The cave was full of gloominess, where only a ray of skylight drifted in from the outside. Under the skylight, Hua Qianyu lay unconscious on the stone bed. Her exquisite figure was wrapped in a green gauze dress, surrounded by the hazy glittering golden light nearby. The jade hairpin was hidden in her beautiful hair, and her face was slightly pale. There were piles of skeletons all around, while the half-dragon, half-snake Monster in the corner curled up quietly, with its round eyes flashing the sad and lonely green light. It seemed to feel the immortal energy emitted by Mu Yunchen, then the Monster moved for a moment.

Mu Yunchen approached and sat lightly beside the stone bed. After the golden light touched the familiar aura, it converged, and the glittering teardrop crystal disappeared in Hua Qianyu's heart without a trace. Mu Yunchen rubbed Hua Qianyu's delicate hands hanging on the sides with great pity, the tips of his fingers slid gently over her slightly cold face, and looked at Hua Qianyu with a soft light and a fine look: full of spiritual energy, steady breathing, but why did she fall asleep? Mu Yunchen considered that through kiss providing vitality, Hua Qianyu would wake up more quickly, but he also considered that although the two of them were in love with each other, they had never expressed their feelings publicly and had never had intimate contact, which made his heart pound.

Mu Yunchen hesitated for a moment, his eyes sank then he leaned down to kiss Hua Qianyu. The fragrance of Hua Qianyu made Mu Yunchen get intoxicated. When their lips touched and the tip of his tongue slipped between her lips and tongue, strands of pure energy passed from Mu Yunchen's body to Hua Qianyu through the entanglement of their two tongues. The soft feeling spread all over her body, Hua Qianyu couldn't help but tremble slightly, unconsciously sucking Mu Yunchen's wet lips and tongue, with her fingertips moving naturally to catch Mu Yunchen's warm hands. Mu Yunchen felt Hua Qianyu's movement, reluctantly left her lips, then gently stroked her forehead, waiting for Hua Qianyu to wake up slowly.

When Hua Qianyu opened her eyes and saw Mu Yunchen's handsome face reflected in her bright eyes, she got up excitedly to hug Mu Yunchen tightly, her head resting on his shoulders, and her heart felt much more at ease. Mu Yunchen caressed her back softly and comforted: "Don't be afraid. I'm here."

Seeing Hua Qianyu had fully recovered, the Monster moved clumsily towards Hua Qianyu. Mu Yunchen saw that it had no intention of attacking, so he moved proactively to the side to make space for it to wrap around Hua Qianyu. And Hua Qianyu looked at the Monster with relief, then reached out to gently stroke its head and back over and over again. The Monster responded with a slender red tongue to lightly lick Hua Qianyu's cheek. There is an inexplicable comfort between one person and one monster.

Hua Qianyu smiled and signaled that Mu Yunchen also stepped forward to caress the Monster, then turned her head to whisper to the Monster: "The dream you entrusted to me while I was sleeping is still vivid in my mind, and I can feel the knife-cut pain you suffered. This lawless world has been evil and chaotic for hundreds of years. I understand that you have good intentions and no harm to others. The wreckages here were actually hurt by those evildoers who abandoned them here after injury them. It is not your fault. I will cast spells for the undead here, as well as I will do my best to lift the seal for you, break free from the shackles, and we escape together." After speaking, Hua Qianyu hugged the Monster and wiped the tears from the corner of her eyes.

Chapter 9: Escape

The Monster was originally a descendant of the dragon and the snake a long time ago. It is a rare creature in the world. For hundreds of years, it has been happily wandering among the marvelous mountains and waters, living by absorbing the natural energy of heaven and earth. However, unfortunately, it was met by the ordinary people. In addition to being frightened, they quickly told the ruler of Xianmen at that time to subdue it. People in the world don't care that the Monster is not harmful to them, but they swarm to maim it because of its strange appearance. Later, the Monster was sealed by the ruler's magic power, arrested in the Monster Cave, and it can never be able to fly in the heaven and earth since then. Through the records of secret history, the current Immortal Governor finally found the Monster and wanted to make use of it, adding a helping hand to his permanent position in the Immortal Gate. Victims were captured by the Immortal Governor's subordinates from all sides, and after brutal torture had no life or only breath left, then were thrown into the cave from time to time. The corpses in the Monster Cave are like the mountains, where the resentments become heavier and heavier.

Hua Qianyu looked lovingly at the Monster with its head resting on her lap and soundly asleep. She moved it a little and placed it on the stone bed, then stood up with Mu Yunchen together to cast spells for the undead in the Monster Cave. The sacred wooden whip and the sacred flower whip that flew from the hands of Mu Yunchen and Hua Qianyu played in perfect ensemble, emitting a beautiful requiem and light of peace. The surrounding mountains of corpses slowly melted into dust, and the strong resentments also followed with the peaceful light disappeared safely in the air. After the Monster awoke from sleep, it walked to Hua Qianyu and Mu Yunchen coquettishly. The two of them worked together to cast the unique mana, trying to unlock the magic seal trapping the Monster, but no matter how hard they tried, the seal could not be removed. Mu Yunchen recalled the secret history records he had read that the sorcery of this seal was unpredictable, and it seemed that there was no solution.

Mu Yunchen and Hua Qianyu tried to combine their immortal energy with spiritual energy, and took the Monster away together. However, when they approached the entrance of the cave, the Monster was suddenly tossed to the point of death. The two of them could only take the Monster back to the cave. Hua Qianyu thought for a while, and said softly to Mu Yunchen: "Yunchen? Or you go back to Lingshan to find Uncle Mu Fuzi first, I will stay in the cave, accompanying our little Monster."

Mu Yunchen looked at Hua Qianyu affectionately, without answering, but lovingly hugged Hua Qianyu tightly into his arms. Hua Qianyu continued: "When I was arrested to the secret place, I accidentally discovered that the Immortal Governor had cultivated countless puppet troops in evilly controlling the spirit stone, and he was also constantly sending troops to destroy the various famous and aristocratic families in Xianmen, which may cause even greater harm. His horror strategy is in the process of planning and brewing. You go back to Lingshan, with Uncle Mu Fuzi together, and gather everyone to discuss countermeasures. Even if you can't get everything ready, it is better than nothing."

"What about you? I'm worried." Mu Yunchen said anxiously. Hua Qianyu reassured Mu Yunchen: "I'm fine. Although they can imprison me, they can't get close to me. Besides, now that I have our little Monster as the fellow, I won't be afraid."

Mu Yunchen held Hua Qianyu's smooth shoulders lightly and looked at her seriously. At this time, each other could understand the deep love in each other's eyes. Mu Yunchen said word by word: "My heart belongs to you, and my love for you has never changed. I can't put you in this danger! Or I am here, you return to Lingshan…" Hua Qianyu was touched and choked: "My love for you is the same… But you are the Head of Lingshan Academy, the people need you more. Now the evil has been rampant for a long time, and the world need to return to the right track. We have the responsibilities on our shoulders." After speaking, Hua Qianyu lightly hugged the Monster beside her, and Mu Yunchen also came up stroking the head of the Monster. It was infinitely gentle.

The Monster suddenly danced, surrounding Mu Yunchen and Hua Qianyu, and spit out two crystal clear elixirs into their mouths. When the elixirs melted into their bodies, the whole body of the Monster became transparent. Then it transformed into Hua Qianyu's delicate fairy bag on the waist, and fell asleep after flashing. Mu Yunchen and Hua Qianyu were stunned by what happened just now, yet the elixir's induction told them that it was death and rebirth. Then the two went out, sealed the cave and renamed it "The Tomb of All Souls".

Chapter Ten: Assassination

In the depths of the jungle a little far from the cave, the two figures who were invisible were holding their breaths, daring not to make any movement, and watched as Mu Yunchen and Hua Qianyu flew away. After a long while, they dared to set off and approach the cave that was sealed and renamed, but they couldn't analyze the slightest movement of the Monster or the smell of death. They were very puzzled and could only go away angrily.

The two master scouts went to a hidden place, and invariably received a note from the family of the richest man in Xianmen. The words above flashed by: Assassinate Chi Yanyan; Blame on Mu Yunchen and Hua Qianyu. It turned out that the two were the undercover agents of the Jiang family who had been hiding in the Governor's Palace for a long time. After receiving the task, they quietly arranged the Mansion where Chi Yanyan was located. When he slept soundly in the beauty's bosom, they started from the dark, cut off his breath with one move, as well as even killed that beauty who shared the bed.

Mu Yunchen and Hua Qianyu returned to Lingshan. Seeing they had returned safely, Uncle Mu Fuzi stepped forward with tears in his eyes and was relieved. Hua Qianyu told Mu Fuzi in detail what she had seen and heard during the outing, worrying that current murderous Immortal Governor would use countless puppet troops to scourge the whole world into purgatory;

Lingshan may have become a thorn in his eyes; if the puppet troops came over, Lingshan Academy had to plan ahead and inform the various famous and aristocratic families to unite against the enemy. Mu Yunchen sent people to urgently fly notes to the vast numbers of suzerains in Xianmen, and jointly discussed strategic affairs with all the wise men in the academy.

After Mu Yunchen had arranged all the big and small matters, his uncle Mu Fuzi instructed Mu Yunchen and Hua Qianyu to place the Monster in the fairy bag to the secret place of the back mountain peak, where the natural energy was most suitable for it. Hua Qianyu gently placed the fairy bag on the elegantly carved jade platform, and the Monster in the fairy bag flashed in response to Hua Qianyu's caressing. Then Mu Yunchen and Hua Qianyu each pulled out a mass of mana from their bodies, which intertwined and lingered around the fairy bag to help the Monster recuperate.

Chapter Eleven: Wars

In the huge and terrifying secret place, the Immortal Governor exercised power to control the spirit stone, there were bursts of dark fire around him, sweating between his brows and forehead, and his emotions were turbulent. After the two master scouts disguised the assassination of Chi Yanyan as the actions of Mu Yunchen and Hua Qianyu, they rushed to the secret place to report the situation. The Immortal Governor heard that the Monster was missing, and Chi Yanyan was killed by Hua Qianyu and Mu Yunchen, who was making an unannounced visit. His veins suddenly stretched, and he jumped out of the gate. The terrified two master scouts were smashed to pieces by his rage in the blink of an eye. He made a voice transmission: "I was going to wipe out Lingshan, but now I just let them all be buried with my son."

The mighty and controlled commanders led the densely packed puppet troops to Lingshan, where there was mourning everywhere, and all lives were devastated. Hua Qianyu had sent secret messages to Wei Youli and Mo Xuanxi in advance, asking them to do their part to protect their own clans and lands to avoid the disaster; when the Immortal Governor left his palace, then they would worked with the allies of various families to quell the chaos.

Lingshan already laid a strict barrier, and no matter how the puppet troops surrounded Lingshan in all directions, it was unable to break through the barrier, then they instead burned, killed and looted around. Mu Yunchen and Hua Qianyu followed behind Uncle Mu Fuzi, floating above the barrier to fight the menacing enemy troops, and the disciples under the barrier assisted in casting mana to strengthen the barrier.

But the commanders and the puppet troops were too numerous to count. Hua Qianyu found that the commanders in all directions controlled the puppet troops under their banners. If they could counter-control the commanders to kill each other, then the puppet troops would also fight against each other. Since the Monster gave Hua Qianyu and Mu Yunchen the elixirs, the two of them have practiced for quite a long time. Their mana and cultivation have greatly increased, almost reaching the pinnacle, even better than Uncle Mu Fuzi.

Hua Qianyu and Mu Yunchen have a tacit understanding of movements. The leaves and petals flying out from the sacred wooden whip and the sacred flower whip are accompanied by the stream of dragon-like and snake-like energy shot in all directions, straight into the commanders, like the sharp arrows injected to their foreheads. After being hit by the leaves and petals like electric currents, strange things started, where the densely packed puppet troops also killed each other as the commanders fought each other. What Hua Qianyu expected was to go through this battle, to wipe out all the puppet troops controlled by the Immortal Governor, so as to cut off his evil wings.

The Immortal Governor, who was far away in the secret place found the abnormal, picked up the spirit stone and looked at it for a while, then hurriedly stepped out of the secret place, summoning his subordinates to fly to Lingshan to find out what happened. When the angry Immortal Governor arrived outside Lingshan, he found that the countless puppet troops he had cultivated for a very long time had been wiped out. He was extremely irritable, the dark flames rose from his hands, and he used full forces to split the barrier of Lingshan. Hua Qianyu and Mu Yunchen guessed that Immortal Governor would come in person and lead the main team to wait there. In order to prevent unnecessary deaths and injuries, Hua Qianyu had suggested that Mu Yunchen let Uncle Mu Fuzi take the crowd from the academy to the seclusion cave to hide. Mu Fuzi was not at ease, and after placing the crowd and sealing the barrier in the seclusion cave, he went to assist Mu Yunchen and Hua Qianyu.

The battle between the two sides was indistinguishable, but the main team of Lingshan was seriously hit hard. Hua Qianyu created a barrier for the injured, as well as the swift sacred flower whip shot out of her hand removed the Immortal Governor's subordinates one by one. The Immortal Governor took advantage of Hua Qianyu's vulnerability to capture her and threatened Mu Yunchen: "Right now, I want to avenge for my son Chi Yanyan and tear you all to pieces!" Hua Qianyu coughed: "Chi Yanyan was not killed by us, but you have done a lot of evils." The Immortal Governor ignored Hua Qianyu's words, while waved his hand to throw the spirit stone into Mu Yunchen's chest. Hua Qianyu panicked to watch Mu Yunchen falling, exhausting all her mana for fatal strike. At this time, Uncle Mu Fuzi rescued Hua Qianyu unexpectedly, and fought with the Immortal Governor. In the end, the two perished together in the raging white light and the dark fire.

Chapter Twelve: Unconsciousness

Hua Qianyu watched weakly as Uncle Mu Fuzi chose to burn himself and sacrifice himself in order to die out the evil Immortal Governor, yet she was helpless and grief-stricken, tears streaming down her cheeks. Hua Qianyu slowly crawled towards the unconscious Mu Yunchen, hugged him little by little, looked at the spirit stone trapped in his chest like a brutal fireball, and guessed that the spirit stone was polluted after being controlled by the Immortal Governor. The spirit has been disturbed.

Hua Qianyu tried to summon the teardrop crystal in her heart. When the teardrop crystal sprinkled strands of silver light like spring water pouring into the fireball-like spirit stone, the burning dark fire was gradually pulled away from the spirit stone. After the teardrop crystal purified, it turned into a strong spiritual power and continuously integrated into Hua Qianyu's body.

Mu Yunchen's hot body finally cooled down a little, and there was still a faint breath in his nose. After all, the spirit stone was too powerful, it was a great luck that Mu Yunchen didn't lose his life on site. All Hua Qianyu could do was to try her best to save Mu Yunchen. When her own spiritual power was almost evenly mixed, Hua Qianyu combined the sacred wooden whip with the sacred flower whip to form an icy cloud bed with the vibrant flower vine as the base, where Mu Yunchen lay quietly inside. Hua Qianyu cast mana to rebuild the barrier surrounding Lingshan tightly, and moved the unconscious Mu Yunchen in the cloud bed to the central hall; went to the seclusion cave to open the seal, and let the crowd of Lingshan come out safely; then put the injured with remaining breath from the main team in the Healing Pavilion, and heal them one by one.

Hua Qianyu played the requiem after the battle, as well as the dead souls of both sides were in peace. Uncle Mu Fuzi's mantle was neatly placed on the mourning hall, that everyone in Lingshan knelt down and worshipped. When everyone saw Hua Qianyu in the central hall working silently to save Mu Yunchen, they couldn't help begging Hua Qianyu to take over the position as the Head of Lingshan Academy: "From now on, all of us in Lingshan will obey you." Hua Qianyu was entrusted with tears and promised to work together with all of them. Hua Qianyu instructed them to take their duties and tasks, and after the division of labor to clean up the immediate affairs of Lingshan, she took Mu Yunchen to fly to the secret place of the back mountain peak, where there was also the Monster in recuperating.

Chapter Thirteen: Reconstruction

After all the families in Xianmen learned that the Immortal Governor's subordinates and his countless puppet troops were destroyed in Lingshan, their morale greatly increased, and they rushed into the huge Governor's Palace in the land of the Immortal Governor. The remaining parties who used to work for the Immortal Governor also fought with each other, since everyone wanted to compete for the position as the new Immortal Governor.

Wei Youli and Mo Xuanxi had led their clans to the land of the Immortal Governor and sent messages to Lingshan for reporting the details to Hua Qianyu. After the war, Lingshan was also severely destroyed. Hua Qianyu had to lead everyone to rebuild the academy and rescue the unconscious Mu Yunchen. She could not leave her position to go to the land of the Immortal Governor, so she decided to send a competent team to assist to solve the disputes and resettle the victims. Hua Qianyu called them in the front hall of the main peak, and after explaining the task, she was still worried a lot: "At this time, the land of the Immortal Governor is in chaos. You try your best to protect the innocent people, and each of you must be very careful to protect your own safety." She injected the spiritual power to increase the cultivation into each team member, then popped in a golden lotus flower with self-defense ability to each member's forehead, which can save their lives in a critical juncture.

After longtime of disputes in several wars, the chaos finally subsided, and the position of the new Immortal Governor was finally held by the richest man from the Jiang family in Xianmen, the Suzerain Master Jiang. This result was determined by the co-optation and compromise of all parties.

Some suzerains believed that Lingshan Academy made the greatest contribution and should support Hua Qianyu as the new Immortal Governor, while some suzerains thought that Hua Qianyu was too young to be qualified for the duties of the new Immortal Governor. Actually Hua Qianyu herself has no intention for the position of Immortal Governor. As long as all suzerains in Xianmen are committed to building peace in the world, that it's her wish.

At the celebration banquet, Jiang Zilan, the only daughter of the Suzerain Master Jiang, who was the new Immortal Governor, brought the prisoners from the old Immortal Governor's remaining people up on site, and announced to see who shot the most prisoners with the joy of archery. The various families present were discussing, then the representative of Lingshan said: "The joy of archery is to see who shoots the most prisoners, however, the prisoners have already been punished, and the shooting of this game is too cruel. Our Lingshan Academy is against it, as our acting Head Hua Qianyu has said even if the remaining people are from the old Immortal Governor, if they are innocent, we should not hurt the innocent." Wei Youli and Mo Xuanxi also loudly agreed with the statement from the representative of Lingshan.

The Suzerain Master Jiang has just taken the position as the new Immortal Governor, and he needs to consolidate his power in priority. It is really not suitable to cause too many troubles. Moreover, although Hua Qianyu of Lingshan Academy was not present, her outstanding mana cultivation is unmatched at a young age. A bit in awe of Lingshan, he motioned to his wife to ask his daughter Jiang Zilan to escort the prisoners back, and said with a pleasant face: "Lingshan Academy said very well. I discussed the release of innocent people with various suzerains, but prevent them from forming a party and making a comeback, we still decided to divide them and live in Shibi Valley, which is surrounded by mountains on three sides." Everyone presented congratulation again on this move.

Jiang Zilan pretended to express thankfulness, came to the representatives of Lingshan Academy, and insinuated: "I feel sad for the great sacrifice you have made in Lingshan, why don't you bring Mu Yunchen to my Mansion, and I will ask the best doctor in the world to heal him to wake up." The young Lingshan disciples next to each other couldn't help complaining, and secretly whispered: "With our Hua Qianyu aside, this lecherous lady should stop lusting after our Mu Yunchen." To avoid unnecessary trouble, the wise old man in the representatives nodded and thanked: "Thanks for your kindness. Yunchen will be treated well by our Lingshan, so you don't have to worry about it, Miss Jiang." Jiang Zilan knew that Lingshan Academy would not let her approach Mu Yunchen easily. After being rejected, her jealousy and resentment towards Hua Qianyu increased for no reason.

During this period, Hua Qianyu spent almost all of her time in the huge library of Lingshan Academy, reading the books day and night, even reading through the strange classics in the secret book room, trying to find a way to rescue Mu Yunchen. Lingshan Academy has resumed as usual, and Hua Qianyu has arranged all matters in an orderly manner. Everyone up and down Lingshan admires her, loves her, watching her constantly busy in the library and back and forth between the back mountain peak, with the gradually thin and haggard figure, and always worries her. The elders and the wise men could not bear, to step forward and persuade her to rest for a while; there will always be a way to wake up Yunchen.

Chapter Fourteen: The Remaining People

It is springs and autumns again, yet the time flies. The fabulous mountain are surrounded by fairy mists, the peaks are astounding, the moonlight shines on the flower forest on the edge of the secret place, and the spring water makes a lively ding-dong sound. Hua Qianyu floated lightly into the cloud bed, laying quietly side by side with the unconscious Mu Yunchen. In fact, Hua Qianyu has restored the pure energy of the spirit stone, and also used the teardrop crystal to absorb more than half of its spiritual power into her body, so that the neutralized spirit stone can be fused with Mu Yunchen's body. But Mu Yunchen's breath was still very weak. As for why, she should understand Mu Yunchen's consciousness in a thousand words. He was burned, when the spirit stone fell. Only through the intersection of consciousness of the two sides, he can be awakened. And the intersection of consciousness is an extremely rare and dangerous practice, requiring each other to be in perfect tacit communication, otherwise, they will die if they are not careful. After the intersection of consciousness, the souls communicate with each other; no matter how far away they are, they will be able to sense each other.

Hua Qianyu held Mu Yunchen's hand tightly, interlocking the fingers, concentrating on the communication of consciousness. To Hua Qianyu's surprise, Mu Yunchen's consciousness did not contradict her at all, and he naturally let her in. But in the world of Mu Yunchen's consciousness, the surrounding area is full of red fire. The land is dry and smoking, no grass grows, only an inch of soil in the middle grows a grand lotus, and Mu Yunchen is lying on the wide lotus leaf, leaning on the lotus flower. Hua Qianyu's heart was hurt like cut by a knife. She hurriedly waved her spiritual energy to turn into bursts of rain, extinguishing the red fire, then the ground under her feet was moistened with wisps of fragrance. Hua Qianyu came out from the lotus flower and slowly approached Mu Yunchen. He was still so elegant and handsome, but his tall body was hot. Hua Qianyu saw Mu Yunchen saying softly: "You are here. I have been waiting for you." Hua Qianyu replied in a trembling voice: "I'm sorry… I'm late…" Mu Yunchen didn't wait for her to finish speaking, he put his forefinger lightly on her baby-like pouted mouth with a "shhh" sound, then picked up her delicate face and kissed. When the two were skin-to-skin, the surrounding land was sprouting like a sky full of stars.

Hua Qianyu woke up from the intersection of consciousness and felt like the legendary dual cultivation. Her body's spiritual power was not reduced, but she was more abundant. Even her cultivation level was rising, and she could feel Mu Yunchen's improvement all the time. The mood is suddenly cheerful and comfortable. After floating down from the cloud bed, Hua Qianyu ran to the jade platform with great joy, kissed the Monster in the fairy bag playfully and said: "Yunchen is saved. Our little Monster should also practice well, and please don't be lazy!" Then she waved her hand and turned away by flying off the mountain peaks.

Wei Youli and Mo Xuanxi came to Lingshan to visit Hua Qianyu. After meeting the elders of Lingshan, they were led to Hua Qianyu by someone. When the three of them met, Wei Youli wanted to hug Hua Qianyu excitedly: "Sister Qianyu, I miss you!" Mo Xuanxi rolled her eyes and grabbed Wei Youli's back collar: "Don't play, but talk to Qianyu about the serious business." Then Hua Qianyu learned that the new Immortal Governor's family seemed to be secretly using the innocent remnants of the old Immortal Governor in Shibi Valley to conduct experiments, and every batch of people who are pulled away has no return. Hua Qianyu said with a heavy face: "In order not to act rashly and alert the enemy, let's dive into the Shibi Valley to find out." Hua Qianyu took Wei Youli and Mo Xuanxi to visit the recovering Mu Yunchen and the Monster, then reinforced the barrier seal on the secret place and the back mountain peak before leaving.

When the three of them arrived at Shibi Valley, they happened to see the overseers taking away batches of ragged and emaciated people, brutally whipping them to the point of being bloody. Hua Qianyu sternly cast spells to stop the atrocities, and asked the supervisors to tell what kind of evil experiment this was. The supervisors took Hua Qianyu to the Mass Grave without saying a word. Hua Qianyu used spiritual power to resuscitate those who were still with breath from the corpses. When the supervisors saw this, they ran away in fright. Hua Qianyu cast spells again to let them can't move: "You have to regret your crimes and go all day long." After speaking, all the remaining people, men, women, elders and children, in Shibi Valley were called to leave here by the three of them and return to the land of the old Immortal Governor. After listening to the report from the subordinates about what Hua Qianyu had done, the new Immortal Governor and his wife smashed the table angrily. However, they also knew that they already did the evil deeds and they were also no match for Hua Qianyu, so they could only calm down.

Chapter 15: Teaching

Jiang Zilan, the only daughter of the new Immortal Governor, said slowly by the side: "Dad and Mom, I have tested my evilly power well, and it is useless to keep those wastes in Shibi Valley. Since Hua Qianyu is so stupid, at this point, why don't we declare to the public that it is Dad's mercifulness and amnesty for the remnants of the old Immortal Governor to allow them return to their land." The new Immortal Governor and his wife hurriedly praised their daughter for her cleverness, then ordered the servants to follow the instructions. When Wei Youli and Mo Xuanxi saw that the streets and alleys were widely covered with flattering announcements praising the kindness of the new Immortal Governor and the new Immortal Governor did not forget to slander Hua Qianyu, they immediately became furious: "This old fox is shameless!"

Hua Qianyu turned a blind eye to the tricky actions of the new Immortal Governor, that her most concern was about how to properly accommodate this large number of all the remaining people. The land of the old Immortal Governor was like the Purgatory. After the melee and looting, the dazzling palaces that used to be extremely extravagant were no longer existed, only the ruins left. Hua Qianyu split a piece of pure place for the remnants to stay, where Wei Youli, Mo Xuanxi and the disciples of Lingshan helped the remnants to rebuild their homes. In order to prevent the remnants from being invaded by evil spirits, Hua Qianyu used her spiritual power to dance the sacred flower whip. When the sparkling petals accompanied by aura bloomed infinitely over the whole land of the old Immortal Governor, a peaceful requiem sounded melodiously, and the resentful souls formed into cumulus clouds. Gradually, the cumulus clouds dissipated, the sun shined all over the land, and everything was as peaceful as ever. Hua Qianyu concisely built a big boundary monument in the center of the land with inscriptions on casting spells to warn all the remaining people and their descendants to choose what is right. She taught them knowledge and wisdom, taught them skills and abilities, and taught them how to grow flowers and herbs, then how to practice as doctors to save people.

All the remaining people were grateful for Hua Qianyu's
willingness to rescue them from the hell Shibi Valley, as well
as gave them a way to rebuild their homes and make a living.
They knelt and kowtowed to Hua Qianyu with tears in their
eyes: "We and our future generations will definitely remember
our benefactor's teachings, choose the good and follow the
doctor's benevolent heart." Hua Qianyu asked everyone to
stand up quickly, then created a protected barrier for the whole
land, at end softly to bid farewell.

There are many rumors in the streets and alleys about Hua
Qianyu, the young female acting Head of Lingshan Academy.
Some say that she is an incarnation of a fairy god who can
bring people back to life, while some say that she is an unruly
female demon who is even worse than the old Immortal
Governor. In addition, the new Immortal Governor deliberately
or unintentionally spread rumors that were unfavorable to Hua
Qianyu in all corners of the world, as well as the storytelling
venues were often full of various guests who commented on
her indiscriminately.

It can be said that after the war against the old Immortal
Governor and the peace and tranquility of the living, the people
of the world are very fond of the young beauty Hua Qianyu.
The various famous and aristocratic families are even more
yearning Lingshan than before, as they fight to grab the chance
to go to Lingshan Academy to seek knowledge.

Hua Qianyu discussed with everyone in Lingshan that there has
been hundreds of years of chaos in the world. As the disciples
of Lingshan, it is indeed the responsibility for them to uphold
the right path. Hua Qianyu said: "The tangible body is always
fragile and fleeting, but the intangible faith can last forever.
Our faith: to walk with the righteous rules of heaven and earth,

to create the well prosperity for the world. Meet the people who are ignorant, teach them; Meet the people who do evils, punish them; Meet the people who struggle in poverty and misfortune, help them."

Hua Qianyu carried out rectification and improvement of Lingshan Academy, and dispatch the learning successful disciples to run schools and teach in various places in the private sector, so that the team of Lingshan Academy would grow, the power of faith would take root and grow too. Everyone was amazed and admired Hua Qianyu's ability to act steadily and resolutely. This would not only solve the problem of the numerous famous and aristocratic families in Xianmen rushing to Lingshan, but also allow the vast common and ordinary civilians to study. Before each disciple leaving the mountains Lingshan, Hua Qianyu will inject a lotus flower with spiritual power in front of their forehead to help them cultivate themselves and prevent danger.

Chapter 16: Lost Infants

In a blink of an eye, many years have passed. Whenever Hua Qianyu has free time, she likes staying in the secret place of the back mountain peak, sometimes running to the jade platform to tease the lazy Monster in the fairy bag, sometimes floating into the cloud bed to nest in Mu Yunchen's arms and whispering to him. Mu Yunchen's breath has returned to normal, and the spirit stone has completely merged with him.

Hua Qianyu laid obediently next to Mu Yunchen as usual, turning over and twisting her slim and graceful figure from time to time, bending her hands to support her face, blinking her smart eyes, and scrutinizing Mu Yunchen, who was sleeping peacefully with his eyes closed. Suddenly she felt a sense of reassurance, then entered into the intersection of consciousness again. At this time, the world of Mu Yunchen's consciousness has undergone earth-shaking changes, which it is better than a fairyland. Lush forests, abundant birds and flowers; colorful lawns, silver butterflies; waterfalls flying down, clear and flowing. Surrounded by immortal energy, the beloved person in the heart is on the side of the lake. Mu Yunchen came from the lake as handsome as an immortal god, smiled and whispered: "Qianyu, come here." He took Hua Qianyu into his arms with affection. The lake is like a warm spring, the water is rippling, and the fragrance of green leaves is floating. After the two of them took an intimate bath, Mu Yunchen gently picked up Hua Qianyu and tenderly placed her on the jade bed. Like the lingering clouds and rain, the two affectionately embraced each other to sleep.

Hua Qianyu sat up from the cloud bed, picked a branch from the vibrant flower vine at the bottom, drew blood from her and Mu Yunchen's fingers respectively, then poured it on the freshly picked flower vine branch by following the spiritual power to put into the fairy bag containing the Monster. And the Monster was turning around with a bright light in the fairy bag, seeming to be very excited. Hua Qianyu leaned her face close to the fairy bag, and gave a warm kiss to the obedient Monster inside: "Our little Monster will grow to be a holy spirit creature. You can be invisible and have a new appearance."

After leaving the mountain peaks back to the academy, Hua Qianyu saluted the elders and the wise men with joy, then said to everyone like a spring breeze: "The hard work pays off. Yunchen will meet us soon!" Everyone smiled happily.

The expatriate disciples from Lingshan all mentioned the loss of infants in their letters, wherever they went. At the beginning, the local people didn't care, but later, more and more infants were lost. Almost every month, boys and girls disappear, who are all just one year old. Many people reported it to the new Immortal Governor, yet no one carried out the investigation for a long time, and it seemed that there was invisible power deliberately to suppress these cases. The disciples felt that something was abnormal, so they rushed letters back to Lingshan and reported the situation to Hua Qianyu.

Hua Qianyu brought some of the cronies to investigate this strange incident secretly, then finally found that the missing infants were abducted and sold from different places. Each time it changed to a different location, yet eventually it was quietly transported to the land of the new Immortal Governor, Jiang's Palace. Hua Qianyu traveled to the local school run by Lingshan, and asked the Lingshan disciples who taught here if there were any students from the Jiang family studying in this school. The Lingshan disciples replied: "There are many juniors from the collateral series of the Jiang family who are studying here and they are of good characters, but they are not welcome by the direct descendant of the new Immortal Governor." Hua Qianyu nodded to show her understanding, and requested the Lingshan disciples to inquire them for a map of the entire Palace of the Jiang family.

The Jiang family is the richest man in Xianmen, and its Suzerain Master is the current new Immortal Governor. It is really not easy to find where the new Immortal Governor is, since the palace government is heavily guarded inside and outside. Taking advantage of the Jiang family's new Immortal Governor holding a private banquet, Hua Qianyu and her cronies sneaked into the mansions in disguise, quietly separated and followed behind the servants, secretly looking for the doubts. Finally, they saw that the perfectly disguised suitcases with fine holes were carefully carried into the Jiang family's secret place.

Chapter 17: Persecution

Hua Qianyu used her spiritual power to stun the servants in the secret place of Jiang's Palace, and flew into the secret place with her cronies. When the suitcases were gently opened, the cronies were all shocked. In each of the dozens suitcases, there were a pair of round and cute one-year-old boys and girls, as if they were trapped in a psychedelic array, neither crying nor laughing. Hua Qianyu breathed out the spiritual power of tranquility to each child, and after unlocking the psychedelic array, she instructed her cronies to bring these pairs of boys and girls safely out of the land of the new Immortal Governor back to Lingshan for helping them to find their parents. She stayed in the secret place herself, circling lightly in the rooms of various organs, and believed that she would be able to investigate the deeper suspicions.

When Hua Qianyu was exploring an ordinary wall with a bland installation, the organ quietly opened. She broke in, yet its inside was actually a collection of secret sorceries stolen from the secret place of the old Immortal Governor! It turned out that the new Immortal Governor family not only used the remnants of the old Immortal Governor to cultivate evilly power, but also drank the blood of one-year-old infants to cultivate longevity. Hua Qianyu was indignant and destroyed all the secret sorceries, then at the same time, she was shocked to discover that there were densely packed infant bones buried under this secret place!

The new Immortal Governor and his wife sensed a close difference, and immediately rushed over with their daughter Jiang Zilan. Being intercepted by Hua Qianyu on the way, they knew that their secrets were exposed and tried to trap Hua Qianyu with a psychedelic array. Seeing Hua Qianyu was easy to break, after a fight, the new Immortal Governor and his wife understood that they were not opponents of Hua Qianyu. Eerily they hesitated for a moment and passed on the powers to their daughter Jiang Zilan, then both died in self-destruction. Hua Qianyu sighed: "This ignorant selfish and self-serving love will end up hurting people a lot." After Jiang Zilan received her parents' double cultivation of evilly powers, she retreated to her bodyguard, straightened her waist and no longer feared Hua Qianyu. Then she said: "Hua Qianyu, I first met you when I was a young student in Lingshan. You and I have known each other for a very long time. Do you think you are amazing? To be honest, since then I have hated you a lot. Who made that there is only you in the heart of Mu Yunchen! Oh, by the way, Chi Yanyan was killed by my Dad and Mom's undercover agents and put the blame on you to lead the war to Lingshan. As for us to practice this evilly power, it should not be your business. Why you have a finger in the pie?!"

Hua Qianyu replied: "You have harmed innocent civilians, as well as you have already lost your morals. You deserve to be punished." Jiang Zilan laughed like crazy: "It depends on whether you have the ability to deal with me! But I want to see your look, if I lied to the world and told the people that eating your flesh and blood will greatly increase their mana and they will never grow old with longevity, see how those mortals cut you alive and gnaw at your bones, hahaha!" After finishing the speaking, Jiang Zilan transmitted her voice to the external by her evilly power. Among the parties who participated in the private banquet in the new Immortal Governor's Palace, there were some originally subordinates from the old Immortal Governor who later joined to the new Immortal Governor not only without punishment but also in robbing together. They all rushed out and surrounded Hua Qianyu, revealing their greedy and ugly faces.

In order to prevent Jiang Zilan from doing evils again, Hua Qianyu with spiritual power trapped Jiang Zilan and her bodyguard in the seal, then leaped up and tried to leave. But through Jiang Zilan's voice transmission announcement, more and more people with evil thoughts rushed to surround Hua Qianyu. When the disciples of Lingshan learned the news, they along with Wei Youli clans and Mo Xuanxi clans came to help Hua Qianyu, and other conscientious people from the various families also wanted to do their best to help. Hua Qianyu worried if the melee started, there would be countless casualties. She flew to the air above the Jiang family's mansions, told everyone not to worry about her and quickly retreat behind the Lingshan disciples to avoid disaster, and let the evildoers fight for her flesh and blood despite the bursts. Hua Qianyu used her spiritual power to protect innocent people, as well as planned to wipe out all the evildoers.

Mu Yunchen appeared and guarded Hua Qianyu with immortal power, where everyone was extremely surprised. The evildoers were even more crazy, frantically believing if they can eat both of them, they would be invincible in the world. Hua Qianyu cooperated with Mu Yunchen to fight. When the last group of evildoers was wiped out, Mu Yunchen said to Jiang Zilan: "You are obsessed, always occupying things that don't belong to you, result in killing yourself." Jiang Zilan said heartlessly: "If I die, Hua Qianyu has to die too!" By taking the opportunity to commit suicide, she gathered the thick black evil spirits and devoured Hua Qianyu.

Chapter Eighteen: Meet Again

Her bodyguard beside Jiang Zilan saw that she had lost her breath and had no ability to make her alive, so he also killed himself without lingering, hugged her body and jumped into the double grave that seemed to be dug just now. The thick earth collapsed, where they both were buried deep. The densely packed corpses of infants under the ghastly ground raised rounds of resentment, then flew to the surroundings of Hua Qianyu to offset the thick black evil spirits that devoured Hua Qianyu. And Hua Qianyu, who was heavily guarded by golden light, slowly lifted into the sky. Countless colorful petals blooming from her body, the silver-like crystal mana descended in all directions with these countless scattered flowers. A sound of the voice from nature coming harmoniously, the world is like a rebirth after a catastrophe, everything is full of vitality, the sun is bright, and the air is clear, with a scene of peace and prosperity. Hua Qianyu floated to the horizon then went with the light.

A delicate budding lotus flower gently fell on Mu Yunchen's palm, and Mu Yunchen smiled softly at it. Since then, there has been a new version of the rumors about Hua Qianyu in the world. They all say that she is a fairy god who descended to earth to eliminate harm for the people and protect the world's peace. The various families over the world have recommended Mu Yunchen to serve as Immortal Governor, and Lingshan Academy also keep in mind inheriting the faith of Hua Qianyu. The remnants of the old Immortal Governor are working diligently and solemnly on the way of doctors; the younger generation of the Jiang family is committed to charity, helping the poor and the weak as well as helping to build the Lingshan branch schools. Wei Youli and Mo Xuanxi finally tied the knot and vowed to have three children, regardless of gender to name them as: Wei Mohua, Wei Moqian, and Wei Moyu, to remember Hua Qianyu. People in Lingshan often cherish and look forward: When will Hua Qianyu return?

Mu Yunchen walked into the secret place of the back mountain peak, as well as looked at the cloud bed held up by the flower vines, recalling the bits and pieces that intersected with Hua Qianyu's consciousness like a dream. He came to the fairy bag and said softly: "Our little Monster, it's getting late, and we need to hurry up to see Qianyu." The Monster in the fairy bag has been elevated to a holy spirit creature, sticking out its naughty head and leaping out with shaking its head and tail. It followed happily behind Mu Yunchen.

The Monster is really like what Hua Qianyu said, its appearance has changed, pink and tender, the whole body is decorated with flowers and green leaves, and it also has a light halo. The two round eyes no longer emit the green light, and it can be changed according to the mood: it is rainbow color when happy, yet it is lake blue color when upset. The slender tongue has also changed from the previous red to a bright and lovely pink. The Monster also can be invisible when it doesn't want to be seen.

One immortal and one spirit flew over the mountains and rivers, then came to an unknown and beautiful island. Mu Yunchen pulled aside the rich clouds and mists, where he saw that the blooming lotus lake was even more beautiful than before, and the glazed yard beside it was also even more chic and fragrant. The Monster was surprised to find that Hua Qianyu, who was already a noble fairy, was sleeping peacefully on the huge half-opened and half-closed lotus petals and leaves, then swiftly floated to her in excitement, sticking out its slender bright pink tongue, kissing and licking Hua Qianyu's delicate face and beautiful hair. When Hua Qianyu's aura is fluttering around, her exquisitely and graceful body is wrapped in a light green tulle. Hua Qianyu woke up from her sweet dream, yet found that a smart holy spirit creature was licking her. She happily took it into her arms: "Welcome you here, our little Monster. Your new look is very beautiful." The huge lotus leaves and petals turned into a sparkling teardrop crystal, gradually hidden in Hua Qianyu's heart.

Hua Qianyu chased the Monster out of the glazed yard, as well as saw Mu Yunchen standing beside the Lotus Lake, dressed in white, exuding strong immortal power, elegant and deserted temperament, attractive and tall figure, in extremely handsome appearance. With a smile on his face, Mu Yunchen greeted Hua Qianyu by his affectionate eyes and said: "You are awake…" Hua Qianyu stepped into Mu Yunchen's arms lightly, confiding in a cute and vivid manner: "Yunchen, I miss you." Mu Yunchen's kiss fell gently on Hua Qianyu's lips. Flocks of larks and colorful butterflies flew over the lotus lake, where the Monster also played happily. (End)

Heartbeat Song
Chapter 1: Look in Distance

It's still spring before arriving in early summer, the weather is already hot in Haicheng City.

The sun was scorching and sultry, and the air was filled with a suffocating stickiness. As the core international metropolis of the Greater Bay Area, the most important thing here is the struggling people who work day and night. The towering fashion buildings are blooming everywhere, and the dense traffic is running around.

In the office on the 68th floor of the Bai Group, Bai Xuan was lying on a soft chair. The assistant had just brought him fresh green tea. His long fingers were pressed against the teacup, as if he had just captured a lively business negotiation. Bai Xuan stood up and walked to the large floor-to-ceiling window. His long body under the navy blue noble suit stood upright, making him look taller and longer with long legs. The face is extremely outstanding, but the handsome eyebrows hide a bit of coldness and gloomy, and there is a sense of danger.

On the open-air balcony of the building opposite the floor-to-ceiling window, almost every day during the lunch break, he can see a slim girl hiding in a bench in the corner, with shoulder-length hair, a clear and clean temperament, simple dress, and a slightly immature beauty. Her hand is either engraving something intoxicated, or writing something intently. Bai Xuan seemed to enjoy watching her every day, like a cold poisonous snake hiding in the dark spying on its private prey.

Qiao Yi was assigned to a famous company for graduation practice from the national key university "Haicheng

University". Although she is a science and engineering woman, her love is sprinkled on sculpture and lyrics, and she runs to the open-air balcony behind the office when she is free. Her parents don't mind that their daughter is introverted and loves to play sculpture and lyrics, as it's not a bad thing anyway.

Qiao Yi took advantage of her lunch break to sit on a bench in the corner of the open-air balcony, then took a pen to write a poem that inspired her recently. Not long after, her parents called from Lvcheng City and said cheerfully: "Hello, daughter. Ah, we bought a super cheap new car, and in two days we will start a nationwide driving tour! How is your work practice?" Qiao Yi hurriedly replied: "The practice is very good, and the company's cafeteria serves meals. It's so good that I'm getting fat. You don't have to worry about me. Mom and Dad, pay attention to driving safely. I wish you two's retirement self-driving tour, have a good time, and be free~" Her parents hung up the phone. After that, Qiao Yi still had a sweet smile on her delicate face.

Bai Xuan stood in front of the floor-to-ceiling window, looking at Qiao Yi in a trance, the corners of his perfect mouth raised inadvertently, which surprised his assistant Wang Xiaojian. After walking out of Bai Xuan's private office, he heard the surrounding employees whispering: "President Bai is in a good mood recently, could it be that the Ten Thousand Years Iron Tree is about to bloom?"

"Hey! You all focus on the work at hand. Don't gossip. When the boss hears, he will increase the workload for you, and you will not feel better." Wang Xiaojian immediately showed the appearance of a foreman and said with akimbo.

Bai Xuan hissed softly in the office, the tea cup at his fingertips was placed on the desk, and he called Assistant Wang Xiaojian: "Xiao Wang, come in." Wang Xiaojian flashed straight in front of Bai Xuan. "Implement these projects to the corresponding departments, and hand over a reasonable draft plan within the next week." Wang Xiaojian was secretly shocked: Really! Just speak of workload, and now workload is here! It seems that employees have to work overtime again. Don't think about living a lazy life on weekends, or go for shopping and watching movies on a date.

The days are getting hotter day by day.

Just as Qiao Yi was about to walk back to the office from the open-air balcony, she received a strange call from the hospital: "Are you Qiao Yi? Your parents had an accident while driving to a remote road a few hours ago. They have been sent to our hospital for treatment, but unfortunately both of them die. You need to come back to deal with the funeral in person. Please take care." Qiao Yi replied blankly with a crying voice: "Okay, I'll go back." The phone slipped from her ear, while Qiao Yi's tears dripped like broken beads. Her face was pale and weak. She was holding back her shaking lips and trying to suppress the cry, her hands and feet were shaking uncontrollably, and she was sitting helplessness on the bench like a panic cub choking, with silent tears wetting the floor.

Bai Xuan saw all this in his eyes, frowned slightly, and took up the binoculars to take a closer look. Qiao Yi was silently staring at the photos of her parents. After a while, she wiped her tears then calmed down, and walked back to the office lonely. Bai Xuan's binoculars were joked by his close friend Zhu Linchuan who was in his office last time. This tall and handsome swinger said without any hesitation: "I said you,

President Bai. You put the binoculars in the office with such sentimentality, are you peeking at beauties or the scenery?"

"Gather up your morals, Zhu Linchuan." Bai Xuan's eyes were half closed at the time, with a somewhat lazy attitude, and he didn't want to talk about this to Zhu Linchuan who had played with him since he was a child. Anyway, he was used to it. Although Zhu Linchuan came from a military family and was a backbone doctor in a key hospital, he would reveal his prototype when he took off his white coat and walked out of the hospital gate.

The next day, Bai Xuan stood in front of the large floor-to-ceiling window during his lunch break as usual, but he didn't see Qiao Yi appearing on the open balcony of the building opposite. He couldn't help feeling a little disappointed and uncomfortable. He turned and sat back in the office chair, lowed his eyes and tapped a pen on the table a few times, but the cold and handsome face showed no emotional fluctuations. Bai Xuan picked up the landline: "Xiao Wang, bring me the printed itinerary." Wang Xiaojian replied in a standard way: "Okay, boss, I'll get it for you right away." In a short while, Wang Xiaojian floated to Bai Xuan's place, the private office.

As the young president of Bai Group, Bai Xuan has high education and high IQ, and his business methods are resolute and precise. However, he is obsessed with emotion over-cleanliness, does not like to be close to women, and has strong self-control. Bai Group was founded by his military-born grandfather. Its business involves technology and fashion products, food and shopping malls, as well as hotel real estate. But when the business came to his father's generation, it was a mess, and the Group had to rely on a commercial marriage to get the stabilization. Therefore, there is no love relationship between his parents. After giving birth to his sister Bai Rou and him, they each had their own living ways in private. About Bai Rou, she is also married through a commercial marriage. The couple has settled overseas for a long time. Even the children are born through the storage of sperm and eggs. Ghosts know how they live.

While listening to Bai Xuan's work adjustment, Wang Xiaojian made arrangements for his business trip, and things were distributed in an orderly manner. Wang Xiaojian has been working for Bai Xuan right after graduating from university. Under the temper of Bai Xuan's inhumane devil for so many years, he has long been a battle-hardened right-hand man in business. Apart from being a bit poisonous, he occasionally has a human touch and is kind of humanity. But Wang Xiaojian has a problem with being a bit pretentious. He always wears a pair of golden glasses, pretends to be a gentle refined rascal, and suits, shirts and leather shoes are concise and neat. He has learned Bai Xuan's way of doing things about 2-3 points, but Bai Xuan's terrifying majesty makes people shudder.

Chapter 2: Accidents

Qiao Yi's mind was blank, as well as she couldn't remember how she rushed to the hospital, how to send her parents' remains to the funeral home for cremation, how to arrange a sea burial for her parents' ashes, and how to complete all the follow-up work. She only remembered that Mom and Dad always said that all things come from nature then back to nature, and they were eager to see numerous great sceneries of the motherland. So as their daughter, she chose the sea burial for them, so that the two elders could travel forward together hand in hand with clear water and clear waves.

Her friend Sun Chuheng accompanied the lost Qiao Yi back to her parents' house in Lvcheng City, however, everything had changed. Sun Chuheng put down the luggage, sat on the sofa in the living room with Qiao Yi, and looked around. Although the sun was shining brightly outside, the house seemed so empty and deserted inside.

Qiao Yi leaned weakly on Sun Chuheng's shoulder, sobbing heartbrokenly. Sun Chuheng, who has short hair usually cool and strong, also shed tears of sadness. She patted Qiao Yi's thin back lightly, while making a soft voice like a big sister, whispering comfort: "Ah-Yi, we are close as sisters, and we will take care of anything together in the future. Aunt and Uncle will definitely love each other as always in the heaven, and they don't want you to be so sad, right? You burst into tears, then you will feel better when you cry out loud. Just lie down for a while when you are tired, and I will cook for you, darling."

Sun Chuheng is 3 years older than Qiao Yi, and the two are sisterhood who met 10 years ago. At that time, Sun Chuheng came to Lvcheng City Middle School as an exchange student. By chance, she and Qiao Yi became close friends at first sight. Later, even as postgraduate student, she applied to study at "Haicheng University" where Qiao Yi is located. Now she works for Haicheng Biomedical College engaged in scientific research. In fact, Sun Chuheng's family had immigrated abroad since her grandfather's generation, but she actually turned back and lived here for a long time.

At that time, Sun Chuheng made countless calls to Qiao Yi, yet did not get any answer. Sun Chuheng was in a great panic and was about to call the police when she received a text message from Qiao Yi to inform her that her parents were killed in a car accident. Sun Chuheng asked for leave from work then immediately drove for almost 4 hours arrived at Lvcheng City. As soon as Qiao Yi saw Sun Chuheng appear in front of her sight, she ran to hug her. The poor crying girl, her tears and snot all rubbed off on Sun Chuheng's shoulder, burping in weep sound: "Ah-Heng, my Mom and my Dad are both no more, boohoo..." Sun Chuheng's eyes were wet but she resisted crying, hugging Qiao Yi tightly: "I'm with you; don't be afraid."

Sun Chuheng worried that Qiao Yi would be sad and sick if she continued to live in this house. The death of her parents was a big blow. Looking in the house, recalling her parents, maybe it would be more beneficial for Qiao Yi to live in a different environment. After all, she has lived in Haicheng City for many years, from studying in university to starting a working career. And this area of Lvcheng City has been included in the new reform project of the local government, it will be demolished and renovated. In the near future, this area will be rebuilt into a technology and fashion eco-city.

The person in charge of the Demolition and Renovation Committee came to visit again. In addition to expressing regret for Qiao Yi's parents' accidental death in a car accident, he also explained to Qiao Yi in detail the terms of the Demolition and Renovation. After consideration, Qiao Yi with Sun Chuheng finally agreed to sign the Demolition and Renovation Agreement, and at the same time got a good amount of monetary compensation. Before leaving, Qiao Yi reluctantly walked back and forth in the house, living room, dining room, kitchen, study, large and small bedrooms, large and small bathrooms, balconies, every inch of the traces left by Mom and Dad has been seen and touched, and recorded by photographs.

After Qiao Yi cried, her emotions returned to normal and she regained her sense of reason. She said softly to Sun Chuheng, "Ah-Heng, my Mom's and my Dad's precious items and photos have been packed into the wooden box, but I still want to bring their wedding dresses and the baby clothes I was born with." Sun Chuheng looked at her and replied dotingly: "All, no problem, as long as you want, I will pack it for you. The rest can be donated, and I will let the environmental protection company recycle it."

The two cleaned up the house, and after everything was arranged, they slowly closed the door. The keys to the house landed crisply on the desk of the Demolition and Renovation Committee. Sun Chuheng hugged Qiao Yi, helped her to sit in the passenger seat of the car, and helped her fasten the seat belt. The warm wind blew on their face all the way, and they finally ran in the direction of Haicheng City.

It has been a week since Qiao Yi returned to the internship company and continued to work. Bai Xuan also returned to the office from a business trip, stood in front of the floor-to-ceiling window, and looked across from him. It was a habitual movement, as well as he wanted to see if the girl reappeared in sight. Holding the teacup in his hand, Bai Xuan took a sip of green tea with a calm expression. The golden sunlight poured in and reflected on the corners of Bai Xuan's raised mouth. The cold and gloomy temperament was reduced a bit, showing a little warmth: She is back, sitting on the bench in the corner of the balcony as usual, quietly, but looked somewhat haggard, and concentrated on engraving the one-foot-high wood carving in her hand, like a family portrait of three persons.

The days are still getting hotter day by day, almost slipping from summer to early autumn.

"Hello? Ah-Yi, are you off work? Come over for dinner today. I will cook tonight, and I will show you my top-chef cooking skills." Sun Chuheng said cheerfully on the phone, "Would you like me to come to pick you up? When can you leave the company?"

"No, no, I ordered your birthday cake in the mall, I'll go to get it after get off work, then take the subway to your house, from the first station to the last station. The subway is new, with central air conditioning, comfortable seats, and very low cost. It's not convenient for you to drive, and I don't want to cause you trouble. See you later~" Qiao Yi answered briskly.

Sun Chuheng's birthday is in early August. She has a neat and tidy personality, tall and beautiful. Especially her temperament is so good that she can be a high-end fashion model. She could rely on her beauty to live, but she prefers to rely on her talent to develop scientific research conscientiously.

Qiao Yi and Sun Chuheng are like two ends of a scale. Qiao Yi is about 172 centimeters tall, a little shorter than Sun Chuheng, but her skeletons are very small, her body is soft and exquisite, as well as her delicate oval face is naturally tender. She looks clean from the outside, and her clear eyes are full of translucent agility. However, her personality is relatively shy and introverted, with voice soft and waxy, afraid of strangers.

When preparing to cook the last dish, Sun Chuheng heard the doorbell and knew that Qiao Yi had arrived. She wore slippers, while ran from the kitchen to the living room to open the door. She saw Qiao Yi say: "Happy birthday, Ah-Heng." There was a charming smile on her face, at the same time, she hurriedly took the beautiful cake from Qiao Yi's hand, as well as happily pulling Qiao Yi into the room to sit at will: "Come, you go to the sofa to rest first, then wash your hands. It's very good. We are getting ready for the dinner time."

Sun Chuheng made the three-cup chicken, sweet and sour pork ribs, stir-fried cabbage, egg pancakes, boiled shrimp and abalone soup that both of them love to eat, then put the fruit cake that Qiao Yi bought in the middle of the table, which made people drool. Qiao Yi carefully lowered her head to set the tableware in the bright dining room. In fact, Sun Chuheng's house is a 4-bedroom, 2-hall, and 3-bathroom apartment. It is far away from the bustling and noisy commercial area. The decoration is mainly gray and white, simple and stylish, yet fashionable, which fits well with the owner of the house.

After Qiao Yi set the tableware, she ran to the sofa in the living room to rummage through her bag. Sun Chuheng stopped her when she saw it: "Ah-Yi, what are you fooling around for? Come here and try this delicious abalone soup."

"Okay, I'll be right now." Qiao Yi took the crystal artwork she carved by herself, and gave it to Sun Chuheng with both hands, a lifelike crystal apple with green leaves exuding bright pink splendor, with Qiao Yi's name and completion date engraved on the base. This is her habit. Every time when she completes a sculpture, she loves to engrave a small name and date.

"Wow! You still have time to carve a gift for me at work. This apple is exactly what I want. I am 26 years old. What I want is peace and happiness! Thank you, my little Ah-Yi~ I will wait for your 23rd birthday in December, then I will cook you a variety of private meals!" Sun Chuheng raised her eyebrows and said happily, like a blooming rose.

Qiao Yi was a little bit shy by her expression, and said in a soft and waxy voice: "Ah-Heng, you have always supported me a lot. This is just a little gift from me. You like it, and I'm also very happy."

The two chatted while eating, and Sun Chuheng asked: "Did the famous company where you intern give you a formal contract yet?"

"No... I guess it's very hopeless. After all, I have delayed work because of the death of my parents, as well as there are so many outstanding interns competing together…" Qiao Yi chewed the three-cup chicken, her mouth bulging like a little squirrel eating chestnuts.

Qiao Yi paused, then said: "I met the boss who led us to have an affair, and he wouldn't let me pass the assessment."

Sun Chuheng's two phoenix eyes widened: "Did he do anything bad to you?! If he dares, I will chop his dick off!"

"No, that won't happen. He is a middle-aged greasy uncle over forty years old. He likes those females who are coquettish and flirtatious."

"Well, don't go back to the company's dormitory these few days, stay here, and I'll help you clean up your room. It just so happens that my family members also want to talk to you, the time difference over their side should be in the morning now, then we'll be together to do the WeChat video later." Sun Chuheng said thoughtfully. "Okay." Qiao Yi replied obediently. The two continued to dinner.

Chapter 3: Get Lucky

On a beautiful Saturday, Sun Chuheng woke up earlier. After exercising in the home gym, she walked back to her room to take a comfortable morning bath. With changing to her refreshing home clothes, she quietly opened the door of Qiao Yi's room. From the gap of the door, she saw that the soft Qiao Yi was still sleeping well in the soft air-conditioning blanket. The early morning sunlight poured in from the bright big window through a half-wisp of thin mist, moisturizing the whole warm room.

Sun Chuheng smiled warmly, then quietly closed Qiao Yi's room door and walked to the kitchen to prepare a nutritious breakfast for the two of them. In about half an hour, a delicious textbook-like breakfast was ready, with vegetables and fruits, minced meat porridge, bread and snacks, eggs and milk, and the color and nutrition were just right. After Sun Chuheng finished eating, she put Qiao Yi's breakfast fresh for her and waited for her to wake up naturally, then walked into the spacious study.

Qiao Yi was awake at 10am, got up in a daze and walked into the bathroom for brushing her teeth and taking a shower.

Sun Chuheng heard Qiao Yi walking out of the room, and also stuck her head out of the study: "Ah-Yi, the breakfast is on the dining table, eggs and minced meat porridge warming in the heat preservation pot for you. Eat slowly, and don't rush too much. After you finish eating, we will go to see the reserved flat and studio, then sign the contract through the intermediary if it is appropriate."

"Okay. Ah-Heng, have you eaten?" Qiao Yi asked softly. "I've eaten. Hehe, I got up earlier than you."

Qiao Yi with Sun Chuheng discussed earlier that she wanted to use the monetary compensation from her parents' house in Lvcheng City to purchase a mini flat and a mini studio in Haicheng City. They have already searched the housings online and booked an appointment with the intermediary. The housings are all in the newly established new area of Haicheng City. The prices are the cheapest and most cost-effective in all areas.

Considering that the internship will end in early September, Qiao Yi probably won't be able to get a formal contract. She has to find a place of her own to be a real sense of security. Although Ah-Heng treats her very well, she doesn't want to become a burden, and she also has to figure out what kind of career she wants to take in the future. After all, her passion is devoted to sculpture and lyrics, and she has no complaints to set up a studio to start a business, no matter how hard or tired she is. It is her choice.

Sun Chuheng stretched out her fingers and touched Qiao Yi's pretty nose at that time: "Darling, you have the good idea. I support you."

The two went out around noon, yet the uncles and aunts in the garden community always looked at them differently when they saw them. Not only did they feel that the two girls were so outstanding, but they also felt that it was inappropriate for them to be too close.

Sun Chuheng drove Qiao Yi to the new area, and after meeting with the intermediary, checked the actual housings in detail.

Both of them were quite satisfied, so they quickly spent an afternoon to sign the contract and go through other formalities. The small housing that Qiao Yi bought is a duplex flat located on a high-rise. The decoration style is fresh and chic. She can just get the luggage to move in, which save money from renovation. The sky garden, the surrounding security, are not bad. In addition, the small studio Qiao Yi bought is also in a new building located in the center of the new area. It is a commercial and residential type, that the space is well utilized. The ready-made creative design is warm and fashionable. Moreover, the new area is not too far from the ecological area where Sun Chuheng is located, and there is a direct subway which has just opened. If Qiao Yi wants to visit her in usual, it is very convenient, so Sun Chuheng is also happy.

On the way back, the two chatted east and west. Qiao Yi said: "Orders for sculptures are continually uninterrupted; some poems have been published by publishing houses with strong literature; as for songs, it is also a coincidence that a few days ago, I received a company saying that they want to buy the song I wrote in order to use for their product advertisement. But I didn't contact to this company myself. The person in charge of their advertising planning department mentioned that some netizens recommended me to them, so they went to see my website... Ah-Heng, do you think this is a trick or I just get lucky?"

Qiao Yi stared at Sun Chuheng with clear eyes like a deer. "What's the name of the company? Did they contact you through the official ways of the company?" Sun Chuheng was also afraid that her younger sister would be fooled.

"The mailbox is suffixed with their company's name, and people who call me can also find out that they work there. By

the way, the company seems to be called Bai Group. " Qiao Yi
thought about it and said softly.

"The Bai Group is a big company. Ah-Yi, their new president is
often the talk of idlers. Even the girls in my working place are
paying much attention to him. Anyway, he is the diamond-level
among the rich and handsome." Sun Chuheng was gossiping,
causing Qiao Yi to look at her in a daze: "Ah-Heng, are you
from the Appearance Association?"

"Oh, darling, it's talking too far. The Bai Group should not be a
trick. You know their dazzling Bai Group building, which is
just opposite your internship company. If you have time, you
can go there and walk around. It's clear. When did they ask you
to sign the authorization contract? Would you like me to go
with you, if you're afraid?"

"In mid-September, I can do it myself. You are still busy with
experiments and business trips. Don't worry about it." Qiao Yi
said sweetly.

Sun Chuheng looked at Qiao Yi, thinking her girl has really
grown up. She has gradually been able to take care of herself,
she knows what she wants to strive for, and she knows how to
use the website to manage her own sculptures and songwriting
works. Sun Chuheng can't help but feel very comforted: "Okay,
I don't worry about it. Your Mom and Dad's legacy has also
been spent by you. If you don't work hard, you will really have
to live on air. But if you treat your elder sister me a little better,
I can continue to nurse you. "

Qiao Yi saw that Sun Chuheng was probably moved and happy
for her today, she became very relax, and she teased her from
time to time, like returning to the years when they just met

each other. Qiao Yi also said mischievously: "Well, I can also nurse Ah-Heng in the future."

Time passed by in the blink of an eye, and Qiao Yi will finish her internship in a week.

The boss who was unintentionally seen by Qiao Yi around the office had an affair. As Qiao Yi expected, she didn't get the final formal contract for her. Qiao Yi was not too depressed. There is always a way out, as long as she is down-to-earth and works diligently. She can make a living no matter what she does. What makes Qiao Yi feel very meaningful is that this internship has met a large group of university graduates from all over the world. Everyone shared their contact information and built a WeChat group together. She seldom speaks in the group, most of the time she prefers to be a loyal listener to everyone, and occasionally joins everyone for dinner.

During the last internship, Qiao Yi didn't have much work to do, so she spent more time running to the open-air balcony. Bai Xuan, who was standing in front of the floor-to-ceiling window opposite the building, also noticed how this girl became more and more idle and often stayed on the balcony bench. The last time Bai Xuan saw her there, she was holding two large pots of lotus succulents in the corner, and she was explaining something to the cleaning aunt on the balcony. When alone, she gently kissed the lotus succulents before leaving.

When going through the formalities for the end of the internship, Qiao Yi was called to the office by her boss. In fact, Qiao Yi didn't want to go in for fear of being embarrassed. After a long thought, she bravely knocked on the glass door.

When the boss saw her coming in, he warmly asked her for how she was, and kept praising her that she was still working hard even if the family had accidents. After a few greetings, he suddenly handed a thick envelope to her: "Qiao Yi, although you didn't pass the assessment in the cruel internship competition, I always believe that you are top-notch. This is my personal compensation and reward to you. If you didn't intend to see my affair before, just cross it out of your mind. Life still has to run towards the sunshine."

Qiao Yi understood what the boss meant. He finally had affair once and twice at such a middle age, but Qiao Yi unluckily saw them all. Qiao Yi's character did not like meddling and gossiping. She just thought that the middle-aged boss was not loyal to the family, which made her feel that this person is a little disgusting. Qiao Yi didn't reach out to accept the wads of cash that the boss put in the envelope, raised her face and said calmly: "Boss, I can't ask for this. As your subordinate, I hope you live a healthy life. Maybe your children and your wife are more need your care."

After speaking in one breath, Qiao Yi quickly left the boss's office as if running away, leaving the middle-aged boss sitting in his seat with a blank face. Qiao Yi hurried back to her seat and let out a long sigh of relief. The things were almost packed, and the clerk in the department gave her the file bag of the internship certificate before leaving off work. Qiao Yi timidly said goodbye to everyone one by one, then stepped out of the gate of this famous company alone.

Bai Xuan didn't see Qiao Yi again for several days, where the corner bench on the open-air balcony of the opposite building was empty. Anyway, he watched this girl almost every day for half a year, now that she doesn't appear anymore, he felt a little bit sense of loss. Bai Xuan stared at the opposite side of the floor-to-ceiling window for a while, then turned to look at the photos on his phone that the girl was seriously sculpting and writing on the balcony. He printed two photos and walked out of the door beckoning Wang Xiaojian to come in. Wang Xiaojian jumped into Bai Xuan's private office responsively.

"Go and check this person for me. I will need the detailed information within two days." Bai Xuan said with a paralyzed expression. But Wang Xiaojian couldn't be too calm. This was the first time his boss had asked him to take the initiative to check on a strange girl.

"The boss is falling in love?? Calm down. I must calm down, Santa Maria…" Wang Xiaojian secretly forked himself in his heart, confirming that this is not an illusion, not an illusion! Wang Xiaojian's young curiosity seemed to be out of his master's control, and he wanted to ask who she is and why he has never seen her before. But the words turned into: "Boss, this girl looks so beautiful."

Bai Xuan raised his black-and-white gloomy and handsome eyes: "You go out, and other unrelated people do not need to know it." "Okay, boss. I will keep it secret and give you an answer on time." After speaking, Wang Xiaojian disappeared without a trace.

Qiao Yi returned to the newly bought small duplex flat, paralyzed in the nest for several days without going out, and reorganized the small flat from beginning to end. She doesn't have much luggage, a large box of simple clothes for the four seasons, a large box of books and artworks wrapped with sealed electronic organs and carving tools, plus a storage box for her parents' relics. Except for leaving two sets of clothes at

Sun Chuheng's house, the rest were moved to her own small house. It didn't take long for Qiao Yi to keep her small house in order. Qiao Yi likes simplicity and cleanliness, so she can do whatever she wants. She placed the wood-carved realistic family portrait of the three of them in the center of the closet, next to the flowers and green scenery that her parents liked when they were alive.

In the afternoon of her spare time, Qiao Yi opened the file bag of the internship certificate to see why it was so heavy. When she saw the envelope containing a large amount of cash that she had refused to accept from her boss, Qiao Yi was instantly stunned. Not knowing what to do, she hurriedly called Sun Chuheng, who was still on a business trip, and told her the ins and outs of the matter.

"Ah-Heng, what do you think I should do? Should I return it?" Qiao Yi said softly and slightly nasally.

"Why do you want to return it? Since he is determined to give it to you, even though you send it back, he won't take it. If he just finds out in his conscience, it will be considered compensation for your unfair assessment. Aren't you short of money?" Sun Chuheng was shouting on the phone.

Qiao Yi thought about it and said: "Then I will donate part of it to the charity organization for poverty alleviation. It happens that in the university I have been doing my best to donate money and necessities in the past few years. I haven't donated yet this year." Sun Chuheng giggled on the other end of the phone that she understood her little sister's kindness: "Okay, just donate some of it, and keep the rest to start a business. It's what you got from your hard work, and it's not a gift."

Chapter 4: Check the Details

Before time to work in the morning, Wang Xiaojian came to the company and walked up and down the aisle of the desk before handing over Qiao Yi's personal file to Bai Xuan. It turned out that this girl was the composer of the company's new advertisement, but the boss didn't seem to know her, otherwise he wouldn't be asked to rush to investigate her. This girl is just someone whom the advertising planning department decided to sign after seeing her work on the Internet by chance. She is still a newcomer in this circle.

Wang Xiaojian walked towards Bai Xuan's office with Qiao Yi's details while thinking "this is interesting". In addition to Bai Xuan, the swinger Zhu Linchuan was there so early, lying comfortably on the soft sofa and pretending to be dead. Wang Xiaojian respectfully handed the file to Bai Xuan with both hands, showing a hesitant expression.

"Anything else? Hurry up. When did you learn to hesitate? Do you still want to do it?" Bai Xuan glanced at Wang Xiaojian.

"Boss, Qiao Yi is the composer of our company's new advertisement." Wang Xiaojian said quickly.

"What?" Bai Xuan raised his head in surprise and hummed a question word. "I checked that the girl's name is Qiao Yi." Wang Xiaojian hurriedly added.

"Well, you go down first." As soon as Wang Xiaojian heard Bai Xuan's words to ease a little, he immediately got out of the door and breathed a sigh of relief.

However, Zhu Linchuan bounced off the sofa like a carp jumping over the dragon gate, and asked Bai Xuan: "What girl? Let me see."

Bai Xuan's long fingers pressed firmly on the Qiao Yi file that Wang Xiaojian had just handed over, he couldn't help rolling his eyes and disliked Zhu Linchuan's troublesomeness: "It's already time, get enough sleep, hurry up and go back to your hospital to be on duty."

Zhu Linchuan stuck to Bai Xuan like super glue: "No, let me see who is it before leaving? After so many years, everyone thought that your iron tree would not bloom, and they thought that you had a relationship with me. My poor innocence has been tainted by you all my life, yet today you happened to let me know that you are checking the girl, a great opportunity~ As compensation for me, let's watch it together."

Knowing that he was thick-skinned, Bai Xuan warned him to shut up after reading it and stop talking. "Don't worry. In addition to being sexy, my mouth has the advantage of being very secretive." Zhu Linchuan finished speaking and made an exaggerated gesture of zippering his mouth.

Bai Xuan opened the file and two thin sheets of papers recorded all of Qiao Yi's information, including age/height/ weight/measures, family background, educational background, life experience, work achievements, housing property, etc. Bai Xuan calmly read the black words on the white papers: Born in an ordinary family from Lvcheng City, her parents died in a car accident, and she has no other close relatives; she graduated from a national key university "Haicheng University", majoring in science and engineering, hobbies carving artworks and composing lyrics; no experience of love, introverted and not used to contacting with people, friend Sun Chuheng, with registered studio and promotion website...

Zhu Linchuan paid more attention to the life photos of Qiao Yi: Under her jet-black hair is a delicate oval face, her slim and soft figure wrapped in a tight and refreshing sleeveless white short T-shirt and short sky blue jeans; stepping on light-colored mid-heeled sandals with a small size, she looks extremely stunning and exquisite; her skin is very fair, as well as her temperament is so pure and abstinent.

"This girl is almost an orphan. Her looks and temperament are amazing! Your eyes are picky enough, President Bai." Zhu Linchuan looked at the photos of Qiao Yi and talked to Bai Xuan without looking back. Seeing Bai Xuan didn't respond, Zhu Linchuan patted him on the shoulders a few times with both hands, but was frightened by the cold eyes that Bai Xuan suddenly swept over.

"No, brother, don't get me wrong! You don't need to look at me so coldly and viciously. We are the best buddies for life. Since I was a child, I wore the same pair of pants with you. Can I steal the girl you care about? No, let me talk about it. There is also a woman I like, but I can't catch up with her yet at the moment, alas~" Zhu Linchuan sighed while holding Bai Xuan in his arms.

"You finally have a woman you can't catch up with? You're always like this, even though you're two years younger than me, you're over 28, and you can't rely on the small and sell the small, just loving to play prank with me." Bai Xuan said calmly and concisely.

"Hey! I'm wandering just wandering, but I'm not messing around. The charming me is still very clean and self-love! Although I occasionally talk about love like an experiment, it's just a matter of spending time, and I didn't write it down in my head. Who made me grow up to be so tall, rich and handsome as well as popular with the public, there will always be an endless stream of pursuers~" Zhu Linchuan put on a cute and silly expression, speaking to Bai Xuan.

Bai Xuan was a little speechless to Zhu Linchuan, who had been close to him since he was a child: "Aren't you being so popular? Then why is someone rejecting you?"

"I said you, Bai Xuan. Don't lift the pot without opening it! You don't understand~ The woman I'm chasing is so cool and gorgeous, her temperament is even better than that of a senior model, and she's also a scientific research talent at Haicheng Biomedical College. She belongs to the "four-high" race with high IQ, high EQ, good looks and tall stature, how can it be so easy to catch up. Your baby me is in pain, that's why I come to you early this morning to find the warm embrace from my brother you, to comfort my fragile little boy heart~" Zhu Linchuan blinked and played with Bai Xuan.

Bai Xuan raised his bright eyes and asked with interest: "How did you meet her?"

Zhu Linchuan immediately recalled emotionally: "At a high-end communication meeting in the medical field, there were little sweet and sour bubbles of my love buds flowing around. Not long after I sat down, I squinted and saw a tall and cool short hair woman walked up to me. I thought she was looking for my signature. I took out the pen and asked her to take the blank document and sign my handsome name. When I handed

the signature back to her, she didn't even look straight at me!
She even put on a puzzled expression of 'you have something
wrong' to me, and I was so embarrassed at the time that I
wanted to hide myself under the ground!"

Zhu Linchuan took a sip of Baixuan's fresh green tea then
continued to talk nonsense: "She just sat beside me so
beautifully and quietly for several hours, yet didn't say a word
to me. When the meeting was about to end, I chased after her
and asked her for her contact information. Guess what
happened? She didn't give it to me! She also used the worst
excuse that she had no contact information, then walked away
with a smile. Fortunately, I heard a few cutie called her Sister
Ah-Heng, while I secretly took a photo of her and saved it so
that I can check the bottom and continue to chase."

These two close friends are as brothers, who love to secretly
photograph their heartbeat girls; it seems that there are really
similarities between them, and they can't escape.

After listening to Zhu Linchuan's long-winded words, Bai
Xuan said he understood, then called the front desk to send two
exquisite breakfasts to his office early to enjoy with Zhu
Linchuan. Seeing he had finished the breakfast with relish, Bai
Xuan swiftly told him to go back to the hospital quickly. Don't
be a shameless old humming. His nonsense pursuits made him
forget his job, and Bai Xuan also couldn't start his work
normally. Before Zhu Linchuan stepped out of the office, he
did not forget to be naughty: "Brother, take this girl out to meet
one day. It just so happens that the National Day holiday is a
good time for gatherings." After speaking, he slipped away.

Seeing Zhu Linchuan had disappeared, Bai Xuan held his
forehead with one hand for a moment, then picked up the

landline phone to call Chen Yuanzhi, the manager of the advertising planning department: "Yuanzhi, you bring the finalization of the new advertisement for technology products that you have prepared recently to my office."

"Okay, boss, I'll be right there." Chen Yuanzhi's crisp voice came from the phone.

Not long after, Chen Yuanzhi, who had a neat style, appeared in front of Bai Xuan and handed over the advertisement to Bai Xuan. Chen Yuanzhi was personally promoted by Bai Xuan, since he valued his excellent work ability and eclectic attitude. This time, Chen Yuanzhi dared to use a rookie newcomer and set Qiao Yi's composition as the new advertising song, precisely because he paid more attention to the quality of the work rather than the composer's reputation. His decision was still controversial at the company's regular meeting.

Bai Xuan was paying close attention to Qiao Yi's "Where the Dreams Are", while Chen Yuanzhi was playing the singing version on the side. The style of the song is soft and fresh, washing the soul, just like walking through the vast starry sky, being in a warm and comfortable sea of flowers, and returning to the innocence of nature. This song is indeed a good match for the company's new robot pillow, which can subconsciously stabilize the breathing rhythm and help consumers get a good relaxation. Moreover, the author even shared the song's creative background with the advertising planning department according to the script.

"Yuanzhi, when will the songwriter come over to sign the contract?" Bai Xuan asked with a light expression on his face.

"At 3 o'clock in the afternoon on Friday, an appointment has been made. Boss, is there any problem?" Chen Yuanzhi was slightly puzzled.

"You bring the songwriter to my office, and I will sign it in person. The work is good. Maybe we can continue to cooperate in the future."

"Understood. I will handle it as you ordered." Chen Yuanzhi felt a burst of joy in his heart upon hearing Bai Xuan's affirmation.

"Well, it's all right. You go off first." Bai Xuan nodded to Chen Yuanzhi with a shallow smile.

"Okay, boss, thank you." After saying that, Chen Yuanzhi exited Bai Xuan's private office with interest.

Bai Xuan then half stepped out of the door and waved to Wang Xiaojian, asking him come to his office.

When Wang Xiaojian came to the office quickly, Bai Xuan said to him in a good mood: "Xiao Wang, change the inspection of the construction site on Friday to the morning, and rush back to the company before 3pm. There is no need to communicate with the person in charge of the construction site in advance. A random surprise visit can better test the quality of the construction site. By the way, tell Uncle Li that the car will be waiting for me downstairs in the company at 9 o'clock on Friday."

Uncle Li is Bai Xuan's exclusive driver and is loyal. Wang Xiaojian answered happily: "Boss, I'll do it right away."

During this time, Qiao Yi also made some simple decorations in the small studio, adding embellishments of green plants. She just received a new order, the customer sent the detailed photos early, and the deposit was paid quickly at the same time. The artwork to be sculpted this time is a full range of custom-made live action figures. Before all the materials were ready, Qiao Yi had been busy in the studio all day.

Sun Chuheng came back from a business trip. After several calls to Qiao Yi without answering as the phone was already turned off, she was worried and annoyed, so she drove straight to the building where Qiao Yi's studio is located. When the elevator ding-dong opened, Sun Chuheng rushed towards the studio to ring the doorbell. Qiao Yi heard it, she thought it was someone from the property management office, and hurriedly put down the half-finished doll she was making. She ran out, yet saw Sun Chuheng who was annoyed, then hurriedly opened the glass door to invite her in.

"What are you doing, Ah-Yi? The phone is always turned off when I call you! I thought something happened to you?!" Sun Chuheng couldn't help raising her voice, criticizing this silly little sister who had no ability to take care of herself at work.

"I'm sorry... I didn't know the phone was turned off. You... come in and sit first." Qiao Yi blinked innocently, looked at Sun Chuheng timidly, then ran around to open various carving materials, and finally found the buried phone below.

Seeing she was fine, Sun Chuheng was almost relieved: "You have used this old mobile phone for several years, now that you have to replace it with a new one."

"But I just fully charged it yesterday, I didn't use it very much, and I didn't expect it to automatically shut down after it ran out of power so soon. Ah-Heng, when the order for this batch of dolls is completed and the final payment is received, I'll go to get a new phone." Qiao Yi eagerly said.

"Well, don't be busy. Take care of your stomach first." Seeing Qiao Yi's pitiful appearance, Sun Chuheng knew her must have not eaten yet. So she picked her up, walked outside, and locked the door of the studio, then took the elevator together to the restaurant at the opposite side of the building for meal.

Chapter 5: Meet up

Today is the date that Qiao Yi and the advertising planning department of Bai Group agreed to sign the authorization contract. It happened that Friday was approaching the weekend. The pedestrians and vehicles on the streets became cheerful and relaxed, as well as the weather became clear and refreshing, minus a bit of heat and sticky feel. Qiao Yi continued to work in her studio in the morning. At noon, she quickly took a few bites of light meals, drank some green tea to refresh her mind, then closed the studio door to catch the subway to the Bai Group.

The 68-story Bai Group Building has a high-end and cool decoration style, where the security inspection process is rigorous and orderly. After Qiao Yi came in, she ran to the elevator area and glanced at the simple silver watch on her thin wrist while walking. There were still 15 minutes left.

With the sound of the bell rang, the elevator door slowly opened. As soon as Qiao Yi stepped into the elevator, she heard footsteps coming from behind, and politely helped to hold down the elevator switch. The first person who appeared in front of her was a meticulous man in a dark suit. When Bai Xuan saw Qiao Yi wore in formal dress in the elevator, a ray of surprise from his silent eyes was fleeting, then he returned to a cold and calm aura. Wang Xiaojian, who followed him, with a delicate and capable demeanor, couldn't help revealing the expression "I know you!" after seeing Qiao Yi with his own eyes. He couldn't help but sigh in his heart: He can't believe that this girl is more photogenic than a photo! Afraid of strangers, Qiao Yi shyly tended to hide on the inner wall of the elevator door. She mustered up the courage to cast an inquiring look at Bai Xuan and Wang Xiaojian, while Wang Xiaojian responded with a smile: "Same, to the 68th floor."

Bai Xuan felt that Wang Xiaojian was not calm, and swept him a silent expression of "pay attention to the behavior". Qiao Yi didn't notice this, but bowed nervously and shyly to them as a greeting, then straightened her body and counted the elevator floors silently. Bai Xuan stood at the back of Qiao Yi's side, his eyes melted a little softly, the corners of his good-looking mouth rose, and he carefully observed her red ears and slightly hot cheeks: she was indeed introverted and soft, however, it caused ripples in his heart...

When the 68th floor arrived, Qiao Yi pressed the elevator to open, and humbly signaled Bai Xuan and Wang Xiaojian to go out first. Bai Xuan gave Qiao Yi a warm smile when he walked out of the elevator, as if to comfort her not to be so nervous and afraid. Qiao Yi immediately felt as if she had received the encouragement, and her expression became more relaxed. Even Wang Xiaojian, who was beside him, felt that his own boss had lost the icy aura he usually brings with him.

Qiao Yi meekly walked to the front desk to report her intention. It didn't take a moment for Chen Yuanzhi to walk out from not far away, holding double contracts in his hand. He saw Qiao Yi and greeted her warmly, then led Qiao Yi to Bai Xuan's office.

Chen Yuanzhi tapped on the office door: "Boss, Qiao Yi, the creator of "Where the Dreams Are" is here." Bai Xuan raised his head slightly from the armchair behind the desk, with a soothing smile on his face, and asked Wang Xiaojian to greet them in.

This time, it was Qiao Yi's turn to be greatly surprised, her head seemed to be short-circuited by an electric current, while she opened her mouth and said "ah" in a daze. On the other hand, Bai Xuan came over and said first: "Hello, we meet again." Chen Yuanzhi was full of doubts: "Boss, so you and Qiao Yi have known each other before." To clarify, Qiao Yi quickly recovered from the surprise: "No, no... We didn't know each other before. We happened to meet in the elevator just now. It's an honor to see you again."

Bai Xuan motioned everyone to sit down on the soft chairs at the round table next to him. Seeing Qiao Yi's obedient appearance, he inadvertently glanced at her twice: "You are very young." Qiao Yi was so nervous that she blurted out: "You are also very young." Feeling that something is not right, she can only lick her lips awkwardly, like a little white rabbit, which makes people want to reach out and rub it.

Next, Bai Xuan introduced the structure and concept of the entire advertisement to Qiao Yi. At the same time, Qiao Yi listened very carefully, and was able to capture the thoughts Bai Xuan wanted to express very tacitly. Wang Xiaojian and Chen Yuanzhi on the side looked at each other, yet felt that the two of them looked like the superfluous bright light bulbs; they didn't dodge it, but they knew if they interjected, they would be stared by the boss.

Bai Xuan's voice changed: "I heard that you can also carve. Can I have a chance to ask you another day?" "No problem. You are welcome to my studio at any time." Qiao Yi took out her business card from her pocket, and politely handed it to Bai Xuan. Qiao Yi thought that Bai Xuan was interested in sculpting, her eyes suddenly lit up, she naturally adjusted her sitting position to be slightly closer to Bai Xuan, and talked impressively about sculpting, as if she had an unshakable persistence in her own field. Qiao Yi completely forgot about her fear of strangers, and her whole body seemed to be covered with a pure halo, so soft that people couldn't bear to touch it. Bai Xuan liked the way she was focused when she got serious. He must have been half a year ago attracted by the way she appeared in the corner of the open-air balcony facing him, engrossed in sculpting and writing.

The two talked congenially, before they realized it, which was time to get off work. Qiao Yi and Bai Xuan signed and sealed the contract with each other. After that, Qiao Yi thanked everyone and was about to leave, when Bai Xuan implied that Wang Xiaojian and Chen Yuanzhi promptly stoped Qiao Yi and asked her to wait for a while then went to have dinner together. Qiao Yi hurriedly refused politely, not expecting to be overwhelmed by the kindness of Wang Xiaojian and Chen Yuanzhi, so she could only unconsciously cast eyes to Bai Xuan for help. Bai Xuan came over to comfort her, said that it was dinner time, and everyone would have a simple meal together. He would sent Qiao Yi home after that, as well as let her don't worry.

Qiao Yi saw that she couldn't refuse furthermore, she knew in her heart that they were not bad people, and she also knew how to look after herself, so she followed them timidly. The place for meal is a quaint private garden club in a wealthy area.

Qiao Yi obediently followed Bai Xuan in, and saw that in the spacious garden club, the winding paths were quiet, the springs and stones were unique, and the style was elegant. Bai Xuan seemed to come this place often. After the four of them were seated, they began to order food. Qiao Yi was confused and did not know what to order. Bai Xuan noticed her embarrassment then leaned over to choose the dishes for her thoughtfully. Qiao Yi always felt very restrained, and felt that all this was unreal. When she thought that Bai Xuan was not paying attention, she raised her hand and squeezed her own face hard. "Well, there is pain." She secretly said in her heart.

Bai Xuan saw her behavior was a little funny and cute: "What are you doing?" Qiao Yi lowered her head in embarrassment and whispered: "See if I'm dreaming." After a few seconds, she continued to say sincerely: "Thank you very much for inviting me to dinner." Bai Xuan gave her a warm smile, while Qiao Yi found that he laughed a little more today. He was not as cold and frosty as everyone said. When Bai Xuan smiled with bright eyes and white teeth, he was so handsome that others could not extricate themselves.

During the meal, the atmosphere of the four of them became much more relaxed and natural. Maybe it was because Qiao Yi slowly got to know everyone, or maybe it was because of the delicious food. Chen Yuanzhi showed the interesting photos and videos of his wife and children to Qiao Yi, and Wang Xiaojian also stretched out his head to join in the fun and kept talking about jokes, which made Qiao Yi laugh happily as if she had a gentle maternal aura, while revealing her neat little tiger teeth, very charming, making Bai Xuan get dazed.

"Qiao Yi, please give me your cell phone." Even though surprised at Bai Xuan's request, Qiao Yi gave him the cell phone still obediently.

Bai Xuan took Qiao Yi's mobile phone to take a group photo for the four of them, as for some reason, he put his personal contact information into her mobile phone without any hassle, and added WeChat to click to send the photo, slightly capricious, then gave it back to Qiao Yi.

Qiao Yi took over the phone shyly, not daring to look directly at Bai Xuan. Trying to divert his attention, she asked: "The cuisines here are very exquisite. If they are carved as works of art, I wonder whether there is any infringement?"

Bai Xuan didn't directly tell Qiao Yi that the private garden club belonged to his personal name, so he turned a corner and said meaningfully to her: "Don't worry, there will be no infringement, and I happen to have this idea. You go back and start sculpting the entire patterns of cuisines, then tell me when you're done. The garden owner will definitely buy it at a high price."

Wang Xiaojian and Chen Yuanzhi not only played the role of bright light bulbs fully, but also practiced their ability to observe words and expressions well. Seeing Qiao Yi's puzzled expression, they hurriedly echoed Bai Xuan and said, "Yes, yes, you can carve until it done, then the boss comes over to buy it from you. If the boss is not available, we are also happy to do the errands and come over to buy it from you."

Qiao Yi didn't think about it any more, and said "um" as an agreement. After the meal, the four of them left the garden club together. They saw that Bai Xuan's driver, Uncle Li, was waiting for them in a luxurious and smooth car. Wang Xiaojian and Chen Yuanzhi said goodbye to everyone. Originally, Qiao Yi also wanted to be with Wang Xiaojian in Chen Yuanzhi's ride, but Bai Xuan invited her to his car.

Knowing Bai Xuan's kindness, Qiao Yi thanked him and Uncle Li respectively, and Uncle Li showed a loving smile when he saw that she was such a well-behaved child. Qiao Yi fell asleep after sitting in the car for a while, yet still slept soundly when she arrived at her residence. Bai Xuan didn't rush to wake her up, but looked at the complex buildings where she lived and felt that she looked fragile, but in fact she was able to manage her life in an orderly manner by herself.

Probably still immersed in food dreams, Qiao Yi moved her body a little, unconsciously smacking her lips like a baby then continuing to sleep, all of which fell into Bai Xuan's affectionate eyes at the moment, causing an inexplicable urge to caress her slightly childish cheeks. He believed that he had enough time to wait until Qiao Yi opened up to him. Just like the battle in the business field, no matter how fierce and difficult to capture, Bai Xuan can always patiently control the rhythm until the victory belongs to him.

A while later, Qiao Yi woke up dazedly. "Did you sleep well?" Bai Xuan asked gently beside her.

"Umh." Qiao Yi meekly rubbed her eyes halfway through, while quickly realized that she was still in Bai Xuan's car! She slept so deeply. Qiao Yi immediately sat up like a three-good primary school student, looked at Bai Xuan and Uncle Li apologetically, and searched for suitable words like a flipping book in her mind to express her apology to Bai Xuan.

Looking at her embarrassment, Bai Xuan smiled softly instead: "I only waited for a while. You're sleepy too, go shower and rest well."

After Qiao Yi bowed and thanked Bai Xuan and Uncle Li, she got out of the car and stepped towards the complex buildings. She even looked back at Bai Xuan quietly on the way, until his car slowly disappeared into the thick night, then she turned into the elevator and went upstairs. When she arrived at her small duplex flat, Qiao Yi washed herself in a hurry, then hurried to the bedroom and lay down.

Thinking back to today's scenes, Bai Xuan's figure was suddenly frozen. Qiao Yi pressed her hot chest, not knowing what was going on. Her heart was beating somewhat faster. Before falling asleep, she hesitated, changed again and again the thank-you text message sent to Bai Xuan, pursed her lips and sent it after confirming that it was correct, then shut down the phone and got into the bed.

The next day was the weekend. Qiao Yi woke up and went to the bathroom then continue falling asleep. Suddenly realizing that the phone was still turned off, afraid that Sun Chuheng would have something to do with her, she hurriedly stretched out her thin hand from the bed to pick up the phone and touched the button to turn it on.

The first thing to catch her eyes was an unexpected text message from Bai Xuan: "Qiao Yi, have a good weekend. Are you free next week? I'll bring the whole series of exquisite cuisine patterns to your studio for your reference, and by the way, I will deliver you the engraving deposit."

When Qiao Yi saw Bai Xuan's message, she couldn't hide her joy. She got up from the bed and typed quickly: "I'm free, and I'll be in the studio after 9 o'clock next week, welcome~ I wish you have a great weekend too, Mr Bai!"

Bai Xuan looked at the reply letter from Qiao Yi on the phone, smiled warmly, and continued to browse her studio website.

Chapter 6: Job Offers

Qiao Yi got up early for accomplishing the different orders, she exercised yoga on the tatami in the living room for half an hour, lay down on the small balcony to rest for a while, then rushed into the bathroom to take a shower, and walked out of the house dressed in a light and self-cultivating manner.

In the old-fashioned breakfast shop at the corner of the community, Qiao Yi ordered simple vegetable and egg rice rolls as well as freshly ground soy milk. In a short while, the owner brought the prepared breakfast to the small table where Qiao Yi sat with a smile. If she hadn't had to catch the subway to the studio, she would still like to get another set of this delicious breakfast.

With the development of the business, Qiao Yi has earned money, and plans to recruit two employees for the studio to work hard with her together. There are really all kinds of people who come to apply for the job. Those with academic qualifications look down on the small studio, those with experience are not convinced that the little boss is too immature, as well as some are purely wealthy youngsters just looking for new gadgets to pass the boring time.

"Headache... Recruitment... Trouble..." Qiao Yi muttered to herself, rubbing her forehead with both hands, closing her eyes and resting.

The doorbell of the studio rang, and Qiao Yi walked out with a slightly tired footstep. Outside the glass door was a pair of applicants who looked like rural youngsters, around 18 to 20 years old. The two of them were surprised that she looked so clean and good-looking, but they were a little overwhelmed. The cute girl standing next to the sturdy boy took a step forward and said to Qiao Yi: "Hello, I'm here to apply for a job." Qiao Yi happily replied: "Please come in."

Qiao Yi politely asked them to sit down in the small living room first, then brought a cup of tea to each of them to relax their moods. When the girl handed over her resume to Qiao Yi, she entered the small independent office with her. When the girl realized that Qiao Yi was the boss of the studio, she gave her an honest expression of admiration. Qiao Yi looked at her resume seriously: Liu Qiulan, with a rural residence, a technical secondary school education, majoring in commerce and trade, has experience in internships of sales and art...

The girl looked nervous and flustered when she saw Qiao Yi quietly reading her resume and didn't speak. Qiao Yi smiled warmly at her, trying to comfort her: "You are good, please don't worry. Is the boy who came with you outside from the same school with you?"

The girl was praised by Qiao Yi, minus a bit of discomfort, and spread a big smile on her face like a red apple.

"Li Chunshu, we met at the last job application company. I was bullied at that time, and he helped me. Today he is free to accompany me for the interview, but he is also looking for a job. If your company has suitable position, can you also give Li Chunshu a chance for an interview...?" The girl sincerely begged Qiao Yi, her big round eyes filled with longing.

"Okay, I was going to recruit two employees. You sit down first. I'll ask the boy to show me his resume."

After Qiao Yi finished speaking, she walked out and greeted the sturdy boy with stubby head hair in a soft voice. He sat side by side with the girl, looking at the girl then back to Qiao Yi with an honest smile.

When he heard Qiao Yi's brief introduction: "Hello, I just plan to recruit two employees here, do you have interest to apply the position?" The boy showed a dazed simple look, while quickly took out a neat resume from the washed blue cloth bag that was a little faded white and handed it respectfully to Qiao Yi, stammered and replied: "Yes, I, I am interested, and this is my, my resume. Please take a look."

Qiao Yi smiled and nodded to the boy, opened his resume and took a closer look: Li Chunshu, with a rural residence, a technical secondary school degree, majoring in mechanical and electrical technology, has experience in internships of fitter, drawing and logistics...

When these two rural girl and boy were still waiting anxiously for Qiao Yi's interview questions, they didn't expect Qiao Yi to directly announce their employment, even skipping the question-and-answer session. The two were overjoyed and grateful to Qiao Yi for the job offers.

Qiao Yi understands the hard path they have taken to find a job, and also values their rare kind and honest quality and firmness in their eyes. She just started a studio that needs such talents, regardless of education and experience. As long as everyone works hard together, and keep the feet on the ground together, they can make the studio better and better.

"This is the labor contract. We usually divide labor and cooperate. I am mainly responsible for creation. One of you is mainly responsible for the business of artworks, and the other is mainly responsible for the business of poetry collections and songs. When we are busy, we will need everyone to help each other. By the way, do you both have interest in working with me to learn simple carving? If so, I can teach you. After you get started, you can carve a qualified finished product, and each person will get an additional commission." Qiao Yi explained patiently with Li Chunshu and Liu Qiulan.

When the two heard that Qiao Yi not only offer jobs for them, but was also willing to accept them as apprentices to teach carving skills, they were so grateful that they almost wiped their tears and snot together, scratched their heads, touched their ears and giggled, as well as called out master to Qiao Yi in unison.

On the contrary, Qiao Yi felt embarrassed that the tips of her ears were red, and she felt that she could not bear the title of master, but these two rural girl and boy were rather sincere. Qiao Yi worried if insisting on avoiding the title of master, she will hurt their pure feelings, then said jokingly: "You call me master, how about I will call you Xiao Li, Xiao Liu? Is it okay?" "Okay, master, we will all listen to you."

After the contract was signed, Qiao Yi then said to them: "you will officially come to work after the National Day. I will arrange your seats by the time, in the semi-open office area between the small living room and the small exhibition room. I wish you both a happy holiday."

The two felt that Qiao Yi was not only a good-natured person, but also had better education and talent, and the office environment was beautiful and poetic. "Thank you! We also wish our master a happy National Day holiday. See you after the holiday~" After bowing, the two left happily together.

Qiao Yi was very satisfied with the successful recruitment of Li Chunshu and Liu Qiulan, so she didn't need to worry any more, then continued to rush work on orders.

Qiao Yi summarizes the poems, songs and sculptures she has created over the years. Some poems with different styles have won large and small publishing and literature awards, some songs with different styles have been adopted by the Cultural Office, and some works of art such as clay carvings, wood carvings, stone carvings, jade carvings, soft pottery carvings, and crystal carvings have been collected or awarded. But Qiao Yi is still not well-known in this industry circle, maybe because she is not full of talents, or maybe because she is too introverted and too low-key, who has no intention of packaging herself. In the small exhibition room, Qiao Yi divided her works into three categories: sculptures and works of art; prose poetry collections and fairy tales series; songs and picture books. All placed neatly, chic and elegant.

In the blink of an eye, it's the weekend, however, Qiao Yi is still busy in the studio. Even Sun Chuheng wanted to go out with her, but she was resolutely rejected, so Sun Chuheng joked: "Ah-Yi, you are really a diligent little bee!"

"You don't understand~ This is an entrepreneur's glorious record~ If you are idle, your mom and dad, your brothers and sisters-in-law on the other side of the ocean are urging you to fall in love~" Qiao Yi shot back at her in WeChat voice, adding a cute hug emoji.

"Oh, I'm going to die, when you are talking about this topic again. You know that I used to talk about love but it's just a child's play like an experiment, how can it be serious. If one of us is a man, it would be a perfect match! "

"Stop, stop~ When I was in university with you, people always said that we were a couple, and I didn't see you refuting it~ Oops, I heard that there is a handsome guy chasing after you, which seems to be true~" Qiao Yi spoke in a naughty voice.

"No, It's still up in the air. But that annoying guy didn't come to my working place recently, clamoring for my contact information or wanting to see me. He should be a man with developed limbs who is just passionate for me three minutes. I don't think he really wants to chase after me, and I don't have time to accompany him anyway. Scientific research is more important than man!" Sun Chuheng said confidently.

"If you and I both don't find the right men, then we are partners to live together when we get old~" Qiao Yi was a little absent-minded.

Sun Chuheng knew that her mind was on her work at this time, so she ended the chat with Qiao Yi after sending the emojis of love and little sun to tease her. There, Bai Xuan also sent a message to Qiao Yi, saying that he had something to deal with temporarily and would come to her studio later. Qiao Yi simply replied "No problem" then put the phone aside, engrossed in her creative inspiration.

It was already afternoon when Bai Xuan arrived, and he personally drove his car to park in the temporary parking space of the building. The old security guard saw him getting out of the car, cold and handsome, with long legs and high temperament, which was rarely encountered in daily life. This old man couldn't help but take a few more glances. Bai Xuan stepped into the building with three steps into two steps, and went straight to the floor where Qiao Yi's studio was located.

When Qiao Yi came out to invite him into the studio, her mind was still immersed in her own creation, with a pen in her mouth and manuscript paper in her hand. She chatted with Bai Xuan about her simple and humble small place, asking him please don't mind and take a seat, and she ran to the desk to quickly clean up the scattered manuscripts, then slipped into the pantry to prepare tea for Bai Xuan.

After she saw Bai Xuan staying in the small exhibition room and scrutinizing her various works, Qiao Yi felt as if she was being raided by her university professor, yet her nerves were unconsciously tense until she pursed her lips and pinched her fingers. But she didn't know that her series of silly little actions couldn't escape the man's observant eyes, that the corners of his mouth curved up perfectly.

Bai Xuan took the tea handed by Qiao Yi, drank half a cup, and his eyes fell on a finely crafted stone sculpture of a playful and peeing little boy. He thought it was very childlike, and he suddenly popped up a mind of making fun of Qiao Yi: "Do you have a washroom in your studio?"

"What? The washroom? Yes, in the bathroom. I'll take you there." Qiao Yi blinked and said hurriedly and worriedly, "Isn't it... This tea doesn't suit your taste? I'm sorry for the drink…"

"I'm kidding you. You are so nervous that you're sweating on your forehead. Relax, I won't eat people. Your studio is equipped with a bathroom? Are you planning to stay overnights here and not even go back home?" Bai Xuan was with one hand in his trouser pocket. He grinned at Qiao Yi. His weekend clothes were more casual, no longer suits and leather shoes, but made him look a little brighter.

"The bathroom is not specially equipped. Because the design style of this studio is originally for both commercial and residential use. When I bought it, I didn't have any extra money to renovate it. I only made simple decorations with lush green plants." Qiao Yi said gently.

Bai Xuan picked up the books on the log shelf nearby: "Not bad. Are these poetry collections and the accompanying illustrations all created by you?"

"Umh, including other works in the exhibition room, I have accumulated and created over the years." Qiao Yi replied shyly.

Bai Xuan didn't think that Qiao Yi also had the abilities to write poetry and painting. He was silent for a while, then the conversation turned to his ostensible purpose: "This is the whole series of cuisine patterns, and the deposit will be paid to you first. The completion time is not in a hurry. It will be good if you can accomplish all in two months."

Qiao Yi happily made the OK gesture. When she smiled wide, the neat little tiger teeth were all exposed perfectly, cute and soft. Bai Xuan was indeed happy to see it.

The two confirmed the engraving details and material requirements, and it was dinner time when Qiao Yi suggested: "Last time, Mr. Bai, you invited me to dinner. If you don't mind this time, can I invite you for an easy meal? Yes? Really easy meal, the restaurant just across the building has a good reputation, and my friend Ah-Heng also likes to have meals there when she comes over."

"Okay, then let's get off work now and go to dinner." Bai Xuan helped Qiao Yi lock the two-story door of the studio. They took the elevator downstairs together, and stepped into the cozy and comfort restaurant at the same time. The night is intoxicating, as well as the dinner is warm and welcoming.

Chapter 7: National Day

The National Day holiday is coming, while the streets and nearby attractions are already crowded. In the huge Bai Group office building, the number of staffs has been reduced by more than half, and everyone is busy traveling abroad in groups or at least taking a domestic tour to join in the popularity. Even Chen Yuanzhi, the manager of the advertising planning department, asked for leave early to take his family with him, and dragged several luggage that were about to soar through the international airport. At this time, he was already high in the sky, and it would be in10 hours to cross the Eurasian continent to arrive the capital of a famous tourist destination, starting this wonderful and joyful travel that envy others.

The aggrieved Wang Xiaojian, a dedicated assistant who has won the hearts of the company, is staring at the computer screen in a daze at this moment. His sitting posture is very standard, but his thoughts have already flown out of the clouds. When Bai Xuan's long fingers landed on his shoulder, Wang Xiaojian was frightened to loss before he recovered his senses: "Hey, my dear boss, you startled me by suddenly appearing behind me silently. Excuse me, what do you need me to do now? The little of me can definitely go through the fire and the boiling water for you."

"I don't need you to go through the fire and the boiling water for me now. What a daze you. It's rare to be so free before the holiday. Let you get off work first, otherwise your father and your mother from afar are about to come to the company, crying for the delay of their youngest son's blind date." Bai Xuan smiled in evil charming.

Wang Xiaojian was still in shock, but his mouth was sweet as honey: "Thank you boss for your kindness! Th blind date is even more terrifying than going to the capital to take the exam in ancient time. You saw that the girls nowadays are so realistic, not only asking the men to be nice appearance and tall height, but also requiring them to have good career and big house~ A rare rich single man like you boss, has nothing to worry about, but a humble person like me has to worry a lot about it~ When will I successfully find the right girl?" The more Wang Xiaojian said, the more excited his eyes became. He kept pouting: "Boss, I also wish you to get rid of the single life as soon as possible~"

"Okay, let you go off work, before I change my mind. Also, don't learn too much from Zhu Linchuan. He is too eloquent and sloppy, but he has affected your manners." Bai Xuan waved to Wang Xiaojian in a good mood. Very quick, after saying "thank you", Wang Xiaojian immediately cleaned up the desk, turned off the computer, put the whole document bag on the back, then disappeared without a trace.

Bai Xuan, who was free, sat alone in the office, holding a green tea cup in his hand, and glanced out the floor-to-ceiling window for a few seconds, while Qiao Yi's voice and smile flashed in his mind, thinking that she was probably still busy in the studio at this time.

He guessed it right. Qiao Yi is really busy in the studio, almost forgets to eat and sleep, since she likes herself in such a fulfilling status.

Qiao Yi was originally somewhat socially terrified, afraid of many people. If she can stay quiet, she will definitely stay quiet. Usually, squeeze the subways and go shoppings is also the courage that life has accumulated over time. She didn't like going out especially during the holidays. No matter how coercive Sun Chuheng tried, she didn't have interest, and hid in her own little world to entertain herself.

When Qiao Yi was still on campus in previous years, her amiable parents were still alive and well in the world. If Qiao Yi could buy a ticket, she would try to rush back to her hometown to accompany the two elders, and sometimes Sun Chuheng would go back to Lvcheng City with her too. If she really could't buy a ticket, she'd rather spend the days writing lyrics or sculpting in her dormitory, while her roommates with the others traveled together. She didn't envy them, and she felt more comfortable having her own space. For further studies, Qiao Yi stayed in the library room. Occasionally Sun Chuheng, who came there, would pick up her dress collar and drag her to the postgraduate residence for a stroll, eating and drinking together for a funny remarkable moment.

The logistics are very strong, and the different materials used for engraving have been quickly sent to the studio. Qiao Yi had to spend half of her time on carving and half on poetry and picture books. She received a lot of orders, so she couldn't rest during the National Day holiday. The little bad habit of staying in bed occasionally was cured by the hard work of entrepreneurial passion and even the symptoms. Recently, the publishing house that has cooperated with her well sent her a new contract to complete a collection of fairy tale poems suitable for young children. While creating the content of the fairy tale poems, Qiao Yi completed the accompanying illustrations and soundtracks together, which saved a lot of time and effort for the publishing house. Besides, her previous two story poem series were both very favored among adults and children. With popular sales, the publishing house is more surprised and happier.

When Bai Xuan called her, Qiao Yi was still immersed in the manuscript, jumping up to look for the phone: "Hello, Mr. Bai."

Her soft and delicate voice came from the receiver, as if it had color, shape, and temperature, which smoothed out the intense strands of cold loneliness in Bai Xuan's heart. Bai Xuan opened his mouth, then a magnetic and seductive voice sounded: "Qiao Yi, where are you going on vacation?"

"Is it the National Day holiday… I'm not going out… Just in the studio. How about you?"

"I don't have any plans for the holiday yet. By the way, I will plan to come to the studio to find you, and check your carving progress as well as other works."

"Huh? Okay, okay… a warm welcome. Would you mind if my friend Ah-Heng will come too?" As soon as Qiao Yi heard that Bai Xuan was coming to the studio to find her again, in addition to some inexplicable expectations, there were more mixed accident feelings in her heart.

"I don't mind, since she is your friend. I'd like to have the honor to get to know her." Bai Xuan knew that the Ah-Heng she was talking about should be Sun Chuheng. Maybe she was the wonder woman whom Zhu Linchuan had been chasing after for several months before he even got her full name.

Bai Xuan also sent a brief message to Zhu Linchuan, informing him that he would have a special surprise for him when he could come to Qiao Yi's studio during the National Day holiday.

"What's the surprise? My brother."
"Secret, you'll know when you come, long-winded."

As usual, Qiao Yi went out early to have a simple breakfast in the old-fashioned breakfast shop and rushed to the studio. She was working hard with writing and sculpting. When she was tired, she played the electronic organ next to her for a while, then continued when her emotions were relieved and inspiration came.

It was the morning when Bai Xuan came to the studio. As soon as Qiao Yi heard the doorbell, she went out happily. When she saw Bai Xuan, her clear and agile eyes were pretty bright, like the shining stars. Bai Xuan looked at her. His expression was as soft as the spring water. The atmosphere between the two was very harmonious. Although Qiao Yi didn't talk much and often showed shyness unconsciously, it did not affect the subtle attraction between them. Bai Xuan could find a sense of peace of mind in Qiao Yi.

Qiao Yi showed Bai Xuan some of the finished jade carving cuisine patterns. Bai Xuan felt that the original rough jade material could be turned into a lively and exquisite work of art with Qiao Yi's knife skills. He had to admire it in his heart and told Qiao Yi that he liked it very much. When Qiao Yi heard the affirmation, her face felt hot again that she was happy.

"With so many manuscripts, are you creating a new work?" Bai Xuan approached her gently.

"Umh, the feedback on the two series of story poems released before is ok. The publishing house I cooperated with sent me a new contract to create a collection of fairy tale poems suitable for young children. The manuscript of the content has been roughly completed, and most of the paintings are also completed, but the composed music I just started doing small sections. Could you please help me to see which part I need to improve?" Qiao Yi's voice was as clean as jade.

"Okay, I'll take a look." Bai Xuan said with a smile. In fact, he rarely touches children, except for occasional contact with the twins nephew and niece who are still babies, and he does not know what kind of books children like, but he believes that works from Qiao Yi should be of high quality. One of the two focused on drawing, the other read the draft carefully, which was poetic and picturesque. The noon sunlight poured into the tranquil interior through the bright glass windows, as well as the leaves of the vibrant green plants were refracted with a crystal-like luster.

Before Sun Chuheng came out of the house, she called Qiao Yi: "Ah-Yi? Have you had lunch yet? Do you want me to bring it to you?"

At this time, Qiao Yi suddenly realized that it was already lunch time, and Bai Xuan should be hungry too. Qiao Yi asked Bai Xuan whether he wanted to have the lunch that Ah-Heng brought with her. After all, even if this noble and outstanding man was easy-going in front of her, he was the boss of the big company, and she dared not decide his lunch on his behalf. Not sure how long he wanted to stay in the studio, but Qiao Yi actually liked the atmosphere of Bai Xuan around her. It's like the two invisible nets woven together.

"Ah-Heng, please bring us two lunches. Besides me, there is also Mr. Bai from the Bai Group here~" Qiao Yi was very relaxed and a little naughty when talking to Sun Chuheng. Bai Xuan hoped that one day she would be the same too when do to him.

When Sun Chuheng heard Qiao Yi's words, her reaction was as if she had won the jackpot in a lottery ticket: "Okay, I'll bring you two some delicious food~" After hanging up the phone, Sun Chuheng rubbed her palms secretly, as if she was going to do something: Mr. Bai? Isn't this the young and new president of Bai Group who has fascinated thousands of girls? Why does he see Ah-Yi again and again in half a month? The president is so busy that he doesn't seem like an idler. Could it be that this old iron tree, this cold handsome man, is about to have bloom in spring?

Qiao Yi kept the glass door of the studio open. Sun Chuheng came in directly when she arrived, saw that the cold and gloomy Bai Xuan and the gentle and clean Qiao Yi were together, and the picture of the two was surprisingly good and beautiful. Sun Chuheng involuntarily showed a fan-like appearance with satisfied smiley. In front of Qiao Yi, Bai Xuan was not as cold and unapproachable as the outside world said, but instead showed a softness from time to time. He is with bright and deep sense eyes, thin lips under the tall nose slightly raised, the profile of the face is as perfect as a knife sculpture, the height and legs are meticulous, and the temperament is of self-discipline and over-cleanliness. Bai Xuan leaned forward silently then paid attention to Sun Chuheng's approach, which frightened Sun Chuheng, who was usually strong and neat, and couldn't help shivering in her heart.

Bai Xuan took the initiative to greet Sun Chuheng on a rare occasion and said with a smile: "Hello, I'm Bai Xuan."

This made Sun Chuheng happy, swept away the chills in her heart just now, and responded to Bai Xuan familiarly: "Hello, I finally have the honor to meet you! I am Sun Chuheng, Ah-Yi's best friend like sister. She often mentions you! Right? Ah-Yi?"

Sun Chuheng winked at Qiao Yi trickily and hinted: "No need to say thank you, your sister is helping you~"

When Qiao Yi was hinted by Sun Chuheng, she was at a loss for words, her delicate face and ears were flushed, and she even doubted that she could spark at this time. So she quickly explained to Bai Xuan shyly and softly: "Mr. Bai, Ah-Heng was just talking nonsense..."

"It's okay. Don't be nervous." Bai Xuan comforted Qiao Yi with a smile. Although his expression was calm, Bai Xuan was very happy of Sun Chuheng's help, and suddenly smelled that she was quite matched with his best friend Zhu Linchuan.

If you expect Zhu Linchuan, you will receive Zhu Linchuan! This man was not very formal. Seeing the studio door opened, he didn't even bother to ring the doorbell, so he just walked in carelessly. When he saw Qiao Yi, Bai Xuan, and Sun Chuheng standing together happily chatting, this tall and handsome swinger, he was stunned in sexy chin: "You...you...you, all know each other!"

The three of them looked at Zhu Linchuan at the same time, only Qiao Yi was puzzled and didn't know this person. Bai Xuan introduced calmly with a smile: "This is my friend Zhu Linchuan. And Linchuan, this is Qiao Yi, and the other is Qiao Yi's friend, Sun Chuheng."

After Zhu Linchuan with Qiao Yi greeted each other friendly, he couldn't wait to approach Sun Chuheng with a proud face: "So your name is Sun Chuheng. Alas~ it's so hard to chase after you!" Sun Chuheng forced out a stiff smile embarrassedly in response to Zhu Linchuan. While Qiao Yi, who was beside them, looked at Bai Xuan secretly, then finally learned that Zhu Linchuan was the handsome guy who fell in love with Ah-Heng some time ago. Zhu Linchuan saw that Sun Chuheng was ignoring him, yet quickly turned to please Qiao Yi to tell him Sun Chuheng's contact information. Qiao Yi really gave the contact information to him without hesitation, and looked at Sun Chuheng mischievously: "Hee hee, let you make fun of me just now!"

Sun Chuheng sighed that she should't go out today without reading the almanac, and unluckily she met her headache, Zhu Linchuan. Before leaving, She told Qiao Yi and Bai Xuan not forget to have lunch while it was warm, then walked towards Zhu Linchuan: "If you don't leave, you want to be the big bright light bulb here?" Zhu Linchuan followed Sun Chuheng agreeably and gladly, like a big loyal dog~

Chapter 8: Go to Countryside

After the holiday, everyone started to get busy again. New members of Qiao Yi's studio, Li Chunshu and Liu Qiulan, each brought a lot of country specialties to Qiao Yi from their rural homes, which were neatly placed beside the stove in the pantry and in the small refrigerator. Liu Qiulan's cooking skills are excellent, so the three of them ate all the specialties satisfactorily for more than a week. Qiao Yi is a very qualified young master. Besides, the two apprentices are very hard-working, and they have already started many assistant jobs in a short period of time.

Bai Xuan kept on frequent business trips in various regions and countries, either on the way to catch a plane or on the way back by a plane. From the busy schedule, he squeezed out time to send brief messages to Qiao Yi, and gradually their hearts seemed to be getting closer.

Unexpectedly, Zhu Linchuan and Sun Chuheng were selected into the national backbone medical team together, and set off to the remote areas for half a year of support work. The urban and rural areas the two were going to, was a western county and city called Yucheng City, with a large population, noisy streets, but a low level of education and medical care, located in the downstream of the national poverty area.

When leaving, Zhu Linchuan doggedly got the seats on the high-speed train with Sun Chuheng together. Sun Chuheng couldn't escape, so she could only stretch out her hand to support her forehead silently, secretly scolding Zhu Linchuan for being a piece of adhesive tape, and following her wherever she went. He really was a trouble not only disturbing her brain but also her gums: Zhu Linchuan is with a pig's head "two hundred and fifty (which means stupid)", asking him to keep a low profile seems impossible...

They sit on the high-speed train with a speed of about 400 kilometers per hour. The city high-rise buildings and the rural farmhouses and fields passing by, makes Zhu Linchuan like a three-year-old bear child with a liberated nature, dancing with joy. Sun Chuheng feels that she is like both a father and a mother, at any time need to prevent him from running around, worrying about the rhythm of his annoyance.

"I haven't been to the countryside for many years. The high-speed rail runs all the way from the southern end to the western end, crossing so many mountains and rivers as well as different provinces and regions. The appearance of the countryside is getting more and more beautiful! There are mountains and mountains, water and water, fields and fields. The villa-style houses are lined up one by one. How can it be more enjoyable than living in the city! I want to live in the countryside in the future." Zhu Linchuan said leisurely, as if talking to himself. Sun Chuheng often travels for scientific research, so she is used to seeing the great rivers and mountains of the motherland. At this time, she is sitting by the window, and she is so beautiful and quiet that she is immersed in the sea of knowledge, yet has no time to talk to him.

On the other hand, the old rural couple sitting in the other row of the aisle next to them happily turned to talk to Zhu Linchuan.

"That's the country's good policy! We were both born in the war years. At that time, we didn't have food, we didn't have clothing, and our lives were in danger all the time. There were shells flying everywhere, houses were dilapidated, people starved to death all over the places, and we even could't afford to live in caves! I can't imagine that I can enjoy a comfortable and happy life in my old age. The villa-style houses for the poor households were built with the help of the national government, and no one would live in a tiled house any more. There is a rural pension every month. Isn't it great? Well! Now that the building of a well-off society has been achieved in an all-round way, of course, everyone is able to get care from it, and the poor who have been left behind are no longer allowed to fall behind!"

"Grandpa and Grandma, you are right. May I ask how old are you both this year?" Zhu Linchuan hurriedly picked up the words.

"It's over 85 years old. We are coming back from seeing our great-granddaughter in the other province! This high-speed rail is very convenient, and it can arrive in a few hours. You can't imagine there used to be muddy roads everywhere. It was even amazing to see a bicycle in the old time! Boy, I think you are so handsome and tall, do you have a girlfriend yet? Would you like us to introduce one to you? Our western areas are famous for the rich in beauty girls! Look at my old lady, she is still a flower in our village, and she was full of suitors when she was young. Keep going, thanks to my quick hands to catch her, haha~" The old man looked at his old wife with laughter on his face, turned his head and said to Zhu Linchuan.

Sun Chuheng heard that the lovely old couple was going to introduce a girlfriend to Zhu Linchuan, closed the book and looked at them with a smile. The two old people said "Oops" then saw Zhu Linchuan wink at them again. As the old couple who keeps walking on the love road, the two of them that have experience immediately understood: "Boy, the girl next to you is so gorgeous. She is very suitable for you!"

Zhu Linchuan's face was about to overflow with honey, and he continued to chat with the two old people: "Hey, grandpa and grandma, this is my future wife, very beautiful, right? We will be a perfect match~" Sun Chuheng was too lazy to retort him, but smiled warmly to the old couple.

On the way of the high-speed train, there was continuous laughter and laughter. The old couple got off the train one stop earlier than Zhu Linchuan and Sun Chuheng. And Zhu Linchuan took the initiative to help the old couple get their luggage out of the carriage, which made the two old people keep saying to Zhu Linchuan and Sun Chuheng: "Boy, you are really good. Girl, you are very lucky." The four shook hands and said goodbye, then the old couple left the station smoothly with the help of the train staff.

The carriage became much quieter all of a sudden, Zhu Linchuan silently looked at Sun Chuheng while pretending to look at the scenery outside the window, and the high-speed train was still moving fast.

After a high-speed train journey of no less than 9 hours, Zhu Linchuan and Sun Chuheng finally came to the place called Yucheng City. The local reception staff enthusiastically took the two to the dormitory buildings arranged in the county city. Zhu Linchuan quietly requested that Sun Chuheng's and his dormitories should be next to each other, and the reception staff agreed with a smile that there would be no problem.

In this way, the two of them almost saw and stayed with each other every day, except that sometimes Sun Chuheng was busy at the Center for Disease Control and Prevention, while Zhu Linchuan was inspecting the Center of the Health Supervision Agency. At other schedules, the two of them would appear at the same time in each hospital and each health branch for point-to-point personnel training and technical guidance. The main task of their visit to the western area this time is to support the local construction of the professional medical teams, improve the supervision and inspection system, and inspect the health education work in urban and rural areas.

With Zhu Linchuan's character, this person quickly became a group with the local medical youths, and also provoked many young girls like flowers and jades to chase after him. Sun Chuheng watched with a cold eye, making complaints that Zhu Linchuan blossomed everywhere without seriousness.

One day, Lamu, a young countryman who knew Sun Chuheng and Zhu Linchuan, invited them to visit his village. Lamu is energetic and cheerful. He works in a health center in the township. This time, he is also among the teams to accept the professional training. He is sincere and needs to be strengthened in medical professional quality.

Lamu drove an ordinary small car and took Sun Chuheng and Zhu Linchuan heading to the village. Zhu Linchuan was fascinated by the landscape outside and the construction of rural villa-style houses. The more he looked at, the happier he became. When he entered the village, he couldn't help but say "Wow"! His eyes lit up: "Lamu! Lamu! These houses in your village are very splendid! All are so unique! It's exquisite and fantastical!"

"Haha, the design of the houses was previously planned by the government, which retains the traditional and modern atmosphere of the village."

"Oh, the western area is nice! The scenery is as beautiful as a fairyland on earth. I'm not boasting it! Lamu, your hometown is especially suitable for growing herbs. Look at the clouds and mists, the lush green hills, and the crystal clear water!"

Sun Chuheng saw Zhu Linchuan, who was fading away his sloppy and swinging temperament, revealing his original sunshine and handsomeness, which made her feel stunned. No matter how coolly she stayed silent, she knew how she had fallen in love with him.

The members of the Lamu family were very friendly and sincere towards Sun Chuheng and Zhu Linchuan, and they kept asking them to try various farm fruits and special delicacies. Even the village chiefs of other villages brought their representatives to join the fun. Hearing that Zhu Linchuan is a famous doctor and Sun Chuheng is a medical researcher, each of them brought their elderly or children with chronic illnesses to the two of them and asked for help. Zhu Linchuan found the local medicinal herbs from the genealogical records of the village, and combined with his medical experience; he distributed the medicines to the patients with intractable diseases, and let them take it according to the instructions.

Unexpectedly, after a course of treatment, those patients really improved a lot, then they returned to normal after a short time. Everyone looked at Zhu Linchuan, this young doctor, almost to worship him as the god of medicine in the villages. Lamu took Sun Chuheng to see the native medicinal herbs in village, and Zhu Linchuan also followed. When the three came to the gurgling stream, Zhu Linchuan's eyes lit up: "Chuheng, look at this purple stone! Does it look like jade? I think it must be wonderful for Qiao Yi to use it as a raw material for carving art!" After speaking, he turned his head to face Sun Chuheng, who was fixedly looking at him.

"Why are you in a daze? You are so affectionate all of a sudden. I'm not used to it~" Zhu Linchuan changed back to his hippie smile.

Sun Chuheng found that she seemed to be a little lost, and hurriedly retorted: "Piss off, don't talk nonsense, and keep up with Lamu."

Lamu looks dark and healthy, with big white teeth, he is very friendly, a little shorter than Zhu Linchuan, and takes the lead. In the season October here, even though the sun is shining all day, in the afternoon, when the breeze blows, the unique cool air gradually rises from the surrounding of the village. Lamu tirelessly introduced the different medicinal herbs that flourished on the hillsides and in the fields to them. Zhu Linchuan and Sun Chuheng listened and asked questions attentively.

When they returned to the residence in the county city, Zhu Linchuan and Sun Chuheng worked together to complete the plan for treating chronic diseases and the use of medicinal herbs. Special thanks to Lamu and the people in the villages, and together with the healing secret, they applied for a patent protection to the state agency.

In different hospitals and pharmacies at the city and county level, the township level and the village level, the two were surprised to find that a vaccine with a suspicious formula was being used, which had caused discomforts and side affects to groups of people. Sun Chuheng rushed to conduct more experimental analysis on this, while Zhu Linchuan concentrated and secretly monitored the reasons behind the circulation of this vaccine, and formally applied for the suspension of use in various hospitals.

Chapter 9: Babies

Entrusted by Sun Chuheng and Zhu Linchuan, Lamu delivered the purple jade found everywhere in village to Qiao Yi's studio. Li Chunshu and Liu Qiulan signed the receipt, since Qiao Yi just happened to be at the publishing house to submit the completed collection of fairy tale poems for children.

Qiao Yi returned to the studio from the outside, Li Chunshu and Liu Qiulan couldn't wait to show Qiao Yi the purple jade package sent by Lamu from the western poverty area: "Master, this purple jade is very suitable for you to use for carving. "

Qiao Yi nodded and smiled at the two apprentices, picked up the purple jade and looked at it carefully: the texture is very good, the color is particularly bright, and it is a rare and high-quality raw material. Qiao Yi was very happy and thanked Sun Chuheng, Zhu Linchuan and Lamu respectively. Not long after, the purple jade carving artwork created by Qiao Yi was sold on the Internet, with related orders caming one after another, which was very popular with customers. Qiao Yi asked the two apprentices to contact the village directly according to the introduction from Lamu, and regularly order and reserve more purple jade.

As the weekend approached, Qiao Yi sent a message to Bai Xuan, who was still on a frequent business trip, informing him that the entire series of exquisite jade carvings in cuisine patterns had been packaged. Bai Xuan replied: "I will let Wang Xiaojian arrange the final payment to your account immediately. On Saturday, Uncle Li will come to the studio to pick you up and send the jade carvings to my house. Please wait for me to come back and don't leave first."

Qiao Yi was a little confused as to why Bai Xuan made this arrangement, but she still chose to answer according to his wishes: "Okay, I'll wait for you."

Just after 9:30am, Uncle Li came to the temporary parking lot downstairs of the building where Qiao Yi's studio is located, and Qiao Yi went downstairs to pick him up: "Uncle Li, please come in. The two are my studio employee and apprentice. Xiao Li and Xiao Liu, please help Uncle Li to move the packaged jade carvings to Uncle Li's car downstairs, thank you."

Li Chunshu and Liu Qiulan said happily: "Okay, master. Uncle Li, please come to the storage room."

The driver, Uncle Li, thought that Qiao Yi would not go to Bai Xuan's house with him, then his wrinkled and loving face showed a little anxiety: "Daughter Qiao, won't you go with me together? Mr. Bai has told me no matter what, I need to successfully invite you to go to his house."

"Uncle Li, please rest assured. I will deliver the goods to Mr. Bai's house together with you. I'm sorry. Xiao Li and Xiao Liu will help you first. I will complete the unfinished work, then go downstairs and leave together." Qiao Yi said with a smile.

When Qiao Yi went downstairs, she saw that the jade carvings were intact and fixed in the back compartment of the car that Uncle Li drove, and a thick protective cover was being added. Qiao Yi said to the two apprentices in a brisk tone: "You two don't have to be busy today. It's just a weekend to relax, and I've wrapped this month's special award on each of your desks in envelopes. Go upstairs to open it and have a look whether did I make any mistakes? When you two leave, please remember to lock the two-story door of the studio~"

Li Chunshu and Liu Qiulan said happily in unison: "Thank you, master! We want to stay in the studio for a while to practice the carving you taught, and wait until after 1pm when we want to go for lunch then we leave. Don't worry, we will lock well the doors and windows."

Uncle Li saw the three obedient and sensible children beside him, and he was also infected with a gratified smile. After Qiao Yi explained the matter, she greeted Uncle Li's smile, got in the car, fastened the seat belt, and went to Bai Xuan's house with Uncle Li.

Haicheng City is located in the southern region, surrounded by the sea on almost three sides. Even in the coming December, the weather is still as hot as summer. Unlike the western region where Sun Chuheng and Zhu Linchuan are located at this time, the temperature difference between morning and night is large, and there is a feeling of winter quietly early. Uncle Li's car drove more and more towards the seaside. It was close to the most beautiful scenery, the most expensive land and the most desirable destination for the rich in the entire international Greater Bay Area. It turns out that Bai Xuan's home is here. To be precise, his villa is here. Qiao Yi thought to herself: It is not difficult to guess that his home is here. After all, he is the president and major shareholder of the prestigious Bai Group. It's just that herself ignored his dazzling background and dazzling business achievements consciously or unconsciously. Suddenly she felt a strange sense of inferiority.

Although they have seen each other just a few times, Uncle Li really likes Qiao Yi, this young girl with a clean and refined appearance and a soft and delicate heart. He treats her as his own daughter, showing his father-like loving care from time to time. Along the way, the two of them talked more, gradually they talked about Bai Xuan, yet the topic became more and more serious. It turned out that Uncle Li and his wife, Aunt Li, had been with Bai Xuan and his sister Bai Rou since they were very young. Aunt Li was mainly responsible for housework, and Uncle Li was mainly responsible for transportation. The two brother and sister used to live in a large villa with a dedicated housekeeper. Later, their parents seemed to have both died accidentally in the large villa due to a conflict. After that, the housekeeper was resigned and the villa was sold, leaving only Uncle Li and Aunt Li. They moved together with the two brother and sister to their grandfather's house. It was not until after their grandfather passed away that Bai Xuan bought a new villa to live here.

The car drove for almost two hours, then finally came to Bai Xuan's home, an elegant villa located on the green hillside facing the blue sea and blue sky. It is constructed of marble, with the decoration better than that of a five-star hotel. There is a statue fountain swimming pool, the surrounding security is strict, and there are groups of villas with a perfect combination of Chinese and Western architectural styles nearby.

Qiao Yi couldn't help but marvel: such a beautiful and unique seaside resort is really a place where rich and noble people live... At this moment, Qiao Yi clearly knew how big the gap was between her and Bai Xuan, then hurriedly shook her head to get rid of her impractical messy fantasies and held her heart to hide her secret affection feelings...

Uncle Li didn't intentionally reveal to Qiao Yi that Bai Xuan's parents were married for business purpose. They transferred their grievances of being victims to their own children, and they seldom accompanied the two children since they were born. After the death of them, Bai Xuan and Bai Rou came to their grandfather who was from military. The two children also did not feel more tenderness in their grandfather's house, but nearly ruthless high-pressure teaching. And Uncle Li is not a gossipy person, he is even taciturn most of the time. He said so much to Qiao Yi today, he must have noticed that Bai Xuan treated Qiao Yi differently, and he also hoped that Qiao Yi could give Bai Xuan the missing warmth.

Qiao Yi got out of the car and planned to move the entire series of jade carvings to the villa together with Uncle Li. At this time, a kind-hearted aunt in her fifties or sixties pushing a double stroller came from the stone table and reclining chair in the garden. When she saw Qiao Yi and Uncle Li standing beside the car, she happily greeted and walked over. Qiao Yi guessed she was Uncle Li's wife: Aunt Li.

"Are you Qiao Yi? Ouch, sit in the house. Let the old man and me move the things." Aunt Li said cheerfully. Qiao Yi stood quietly behind Uncle Li, a little afraid of the stranger, and answered a little cautiously and shyly: "Hello, I'm Qiao Yi."

Uncle Li introduced Aunt Li to Qiao Yi with a smile: "This is my wife. If you don't mind, you can call her Aunt Li with Mr. Bai." Qiao Yi said obediently: "Okay." Aunt Li took care of the two sleeping babies in the stroller, raised her head and interjected with joy: "Over the years, both of us have always had a regret, that we just hope to have a daughter who looks like you, haha~" Qiao Yi greeting Uncle Li and Aunt Li's gentle and loving gazes, she smiled warmly at them, and felt that the two elders really treated her like a daughter. She seemed to see the images of her deceased parents in a trance.

Qiao Yi looked curiously at the twin babies in the stroller who were sleeping naively. Their red faces were shining brightly, and their white and tender bodies were round and distinct, like finely crafted works of art. Qiao Yi was somewhat surprised and thought: Is it possible that this pair of babies are Bai Xuan's children? But she has never heard anyone else or Bai Xuan himself said that he was married. Looking at the two babies, they don't look like Bai Xuan, and they are not even one year old...

Aunt Li pushed the stroller into the bright villa and motioned for Uncle Li to bring Qiao Yi in with him. Aunt Li gently picked up the two sleeping babies and put them on the baby bed in the spacious and soft lounge. Then the three put the entire series of jade carvings from the back compartment to the collection hall on the third floor as instructed. After finishing the work, Uncle Li went to drive the car into the garage, while Aunt Li showed Qiao Yi a general tour of the villa. Due to the large space, it took a lot of time to walk from the third floor to the first floor. The structural style of the villa subtly integrates elegance, simplicity and richness into one, reflecting the unique essence of architectural art. Qiao Yi saw the well-proportioned floors inside and outside, and the beautiful scenery on each floor has its own merits, which is pleasing to the eyes and never gets tired of seeing it.

Bai Xuan's personality is cold and distant. He used to be the only one living in the huge villa. Now that there are the two babies, and Uncle Li and Aunt Li often stay to help, who occasionally go home in their spare time. While the twins were still asleep, the three of them started chatting happily. It turned out that the twins were the children of Bai Xuan's sister Bai Rou and her husband Xiao Yin. Originally, the entire Xiao family and relatives had already emigrated overseas and took root in the most developed neutral country in the world, where a large number of the population originated from China. Bai Rou and her husband also came together through the commercial marriage. The husband and the wife seem to be disdainful of falling in love. They are both outstanding scientific research experts in the international field. The energy of the both is focused on their partnership research of the "In Vitro Fertility" genetic project. In November, Bai Rou and Xiao Yin suddenly returned to Haicheng City with the pair of dragon-phoenix twins, and hurriedly handed the children to Bai Xuan, then headed to the northern capital of the country and flew back to the neutral country overseas.

The more Qiao Yi listened to Uncle Li and Aunt Li, the more she felt that Bai Xuan's family relationship was mysterious. At the same time, she seemed to be able to understand the various pressures and responsibilities he was under, and she couldn't help but feel a little bit of imperceptible concern in her heart with the understanding.

From time to time, Aunt Li walked into the lounge and came to the bed, looking down dotingly to see if the two babies had woken up and were ready to make milk. With the babbling sounds, the two babies woke up before and after. "Coming, coming!" Aunt Li came happily with two milk bottles.

Qiao Yi and Uncle Li also followed Aunt Li to see if they could help. Although the two children are under the age of one, they were able to get up from the bed by themselves. They just woke up with pink and tender faces, like the bright red apples in the harvest autumn, staring at Qiao Yi excitedly with big innocent eyes. Both raised their little hands that were as tender as lotus roots and asked Qiao Yi to hug them.

"Yo! The two babies have never taken the initiative! They even ignore their parents. We take care of these two little treasures day and night. For so long, they drink milk and sleep when they are hungry and dozy, yet they don't love to hug us! It seems that the two little ones are inseparable from you, daughter Qiao." Aunt Li laughed and said next to her, even Uncle Li was also surprised.

"Maybe the two babies are just curious for first time to see me." Qiao Yi looked at the dragon-phoenix twins and smiled gently, took two milk bottles from Aunt Li, and tried to pass them to the two babies. Unexpectedly, the two little ones are very smart, they immediately rolled up their little hands to hold the milk bottle then sucked deliciously. After eating and drinking, the two babies danced and babbled "yah, ah", trying to get around Qiao Yi and begging for a hug. Uncle Li and Aunt Li helped to move the stroller, while Qiao Yi was also self-taught. She slowly picked the two babies up and lightly placed them on the double stroller, as well as said to everyone with a smile: "Where are we going now?"

Aunt Li answered happily: "It's almost 2 o'clock in the afternoon. I am estimating that Mr. Bai should be home soon. The old man and I are going to prepare lunch. Daughter Qiao, since these two little treasures are so attached to you, then you take them to the garden. Just go around, pay attention to safety and don't go too far. It just so happens that the sun outside is not too harsh. It's healthier to bask in the sun!"

Uncle Li said kindly to Qiao Yi on the side: "Come here. I'll help you take the stroller down the aisle first, then I'll help the old lady for preparing lunch."

"Thank you Uncle Li, Aunt Li. But... what are the names of the two babies? I don't know yet." Qiao Yi asked Uncle Li and Aunt Li, as well as looked down at the lovely pair of babies with soft eyes.

"Names? The boy's name is Xiao Youyou, and the girl's name is Xiao Xiuxiu. Haha, Mr. Bai is their uncle. He is not satisfied with the names of the two babies. He said that they will have their official scientific names when they grow up~" Aunt Li talked in joyful laughing.

"Okay, then I'll take them to play in the garden." After speaking, Qiao Yi pushed the stroller with the two babies and went to the garden.

Not long after, Wang Xiaojian drove Bai Xuan home in his assistant's car. Aunt Li and Uncle Li happened to have just prepared their lunch.

"Wow, it smells so good! Aunt Li and Uncle Li, your cooking skills are getting better and better! Uh! The boss and I were so hungry that we went straight here from the airport, even I didn't have time to take a sip of the full bottle of water." Wang Xiaojian stared at the rich lunch on the revolving table while pouting. As soon as he stepped into the villa, he helped Bai Xuan unload the luggage, and when he smelled the fragrance of the food, he went into the kitchen directly without hesitation.

Bai Xuan didn't see Qiao Yi and the nephew and niece of the dragon-phoenix twins. He frowned slightly, and asked Aunt Li and Uncle Li: "Where's Qiao Yi? Isn't she already here? And Xiao Youyou and Xiao Xiuxiu, where are they too? Are they still taking a nap?"

Just as Uncle Li was about to answer, Aunt Li took the lead and said cheerfully: "Daughter Qiao are already here before noon. The two little ones wake up from their nap then they stick together as soon as they see daughter Qiao, and they don't want us to hug them. They are all in the garden now. You and Xiao Wang have just come back hungry. If you want to eat first, the old man and I will go to the garden to pick them up. Daughter Qiao hasn't eaten anything yet, so she's probably hungry too. "

"No, I'll go to the garden to find them. Uncle Li, Aunt Li, and Xiao Wang, you all sit down and eat first." After Bai Xuan finished speaking, he turned and walked out of the villa, ignoring the tiredness of the business trip and walking towards the garden in hurry steps. When he saw Qiao Yi sitting on the stone bench with her back to him, talking to the two babies in a soft voice, making the dragon-phoenix twins burst into laughter, Bai Xuan couldn't bear to disturb them. His originally cold corners of the eyes have been rubbed into warm light, and a slightly hoarse voice sounded: "Qiao Yi?"

When Qiao Yi heard her being called, she got up and turned to look at Bai Xuan, her bright eyes shining with the joy of reunion after a long absence: "Mr. Bai, you're back~" The twins were also excited when they saw Bai Xuan approaching, waving their little hands and feet.

Bai Xuan stared at Qiao Yi with imperceptible tenderness, nodded and smiled to Qiao Yi: "Well, let's go back to the house and have lunch together." Then the two of them, each hugged a baby in a tacit understanding, and Bai Xuan also pushed the stroller. They went to the villa dining area together.

Chapter 10: Get along

After lunch, Bai Xuan and Qiao Yi took the two babies to the living hall to play. Wang Xiaojian ate a lot and was still nibbling on the sauce-flavored chicken thigh with relish. Uncle Li and Aunt Li hurriedly persuaded him: "Slow down, don't rush, so as not to choke."

When nibbling on the last chicken thigh, Wang Xiaojian washed his hands, and approached Uncle Li and Aunt Li with the pompous mouth: "I love the food made by you two elders. It's like a god of cooking. After eating, I can sweep away all my troubles. Refreshing~"

Uncle Li and Aunt Li replied dotingly: "If you want to eat, we will cook the meal for you again when next time you come to pick up Mr. Bai."

After Wang Xiaojian had eaten and drunken enough, he finally remembered that he was going to do something serious. He did not forget to add some drama, and motioned Uncle Li and Aunt Li to look at Bai Xuan, Qiao Yi and the two babies who are in playing: "They are all together now. Hehe~ the more you look, the more you find from them like family."

Uncle Li and Aunt Li did not refute, but smiled and nodded to Wang Xiaojian in agreement, then cleaned up the dining area and went to work on other things. Wang Xiaojian received the hint from Bai Xuan's eyes, and seriously approached the briefcase to rummage through relevant documents.

At this time, when the smart and cute twins were tired from playing and fell asleep, Qiao Yi and Bai Xuan hugged the two babies and gently coaxed them to sleep well, then placed them on the bed in the spacious and soft lounge, while Wang Xiaojian held the official document bags waiting in the living hall.

Bai Xuan brought Qiao Yi to Wang Xiaojian and said: "Come together, let's go to the office on the third floor and talk about something."

Qiao Yi felt that the two of them were a bit mysterious, yet it was not easy to ask anything, so she followed with a reply "oh".

Bai Xuan opened the closed office with his fingerprints. Wang Xiaojian followed Bai Xuan all the time. Qiao Yi slightly lowered her head and cautiously as soon as she stepped into the door. She looked at the cold and high-end design style around her in surprise. The serious atmosphere was so suppressed that she didn't dare to breathe too much, while her little heart couldn't help but lift.

"Sit down first." Bai Xuan took two documents from Wang Xiaojian's hand, and asked Qiao Yi halfway through the documents with a slow expression, "How was your day at my house? Do like Uncle Li, Aunt Li and my nephew and niece?"

"Your, your house is very nice. Uncle Li and Aunt Li are very good. Your nephew and niece are very cute. I, I like them."

When Qiao Yi heard Bai Xuan's question, she was so nervous that she stammered in reply. With her palms flatted on her legs, she involuntarily rubbed them around, shrinking into fists and sweating silently. Qiao Yi didn't know what exactly Bai Xuan wanted her to do.

Wang Xiaojian looked at Qiao Yi with a smile, as if he was deliberately pretending to be serious. But next to Bai Xuan, he also didn't dare to say a word.

"This is the contract. I want to hire you as the personal tutor for the dragon-phoenix twins, my nephew and niece." Bai Xuan stared at Qiao Yi and handed her the document.

"What... what?! But I'm inexperienced! I'm not married... I don't have children... I haven't formally taught children... I don't think... I'm not competent. Besides, there are still studio matters. I'm busy... I'm afraid I won't be able to take care of them... What should I do if I delay your nephew and niece...?"

Qiao Yi waved her hands nervously and hurriedly, as well as tried to explain to Bai Xuan urgently.

"Look at the contract first. It doesn't matter whether you have experience or not. The main truth is that the dragon-phoenix twins have a fate with you. They have the same birthday as you, and they hit it off with you, so they stick to you. Don't worry, the working hours are very flexible, and you can come to accompany them on weekends when you are free. They don't need special parent-child professional skills to take care of, just following your heart to get along with them." Bai Xuan said intently.

Qiao Yi obediently picked up the document and looked up and down. Even though she could understand all the black words on the white papers, her head was blank to difficultly remember what was written in the contract. Then she couldn't help but ask: "The children's parents agreed to hire me?"

There was deep sadness in Bai Xuan's eyes, but it was fleeting. He lowered his voice and returned to calm, then looked at Qiao Yi with serious eyes and replied: "From now on, I am the guardian of the two children. I decided to hire you, then it is you, rest assured."

"Thank you for giving me the opportunity." Qiao Yi said shyly, and signed her name on the two contracts signed and sealed by Bai Xuan, then took the red ink from Wang Xiaojian's hand and stamped it on her finger to press her own fingerprint. She couldn't help thinking in her heart: The salary is ridiculously high... She is embarrassed to take it. Sure enough, what a rich man. The contract period...

"Uh? Does the contract have a limit date?" Qiao Yi remembered after signing the paper and stamping her handprint, then asked Bai Xuan with clear eyes.

Bai Xuan picked up the contract, handed a copy to Qiao Yi, smiled meaningfully and shook his head, while Wang Xiaojian next to him shrugged silently.

After the contract was completed, Bai Xuan asked Wang Xiaojian and Qiao Yi to go downstairs first, yet he stayed alone in the office with his eyes closed for contemplation.

Aunt Li was busying on the second floor, while Uncle Li was pruning flowers and trees in the garden. Qiao Yi went to the lounge on the first floor to see the dragon-phoenix twins, and found that they were still sleeping, looking naive and very cute. Then Qiao Yi picked up the smart remote control, went out at ease, and followed Wang Xiaojian to the flower corridor outside the villa for a chat.

"Beauty Qiao, our company's new product advertisement created by you has been promoted across the board. Judging from the sales of the Double Eleven shopping carnival, the effect is surprisingly good, and this new product advertisement of our company has been occupying the hot search. The huge LED screen of the company building also played it continuously, making it super eye-catching and becoming a beautiful landscape~ Huh? What is your expression? The song you wrote is so popular now, how can you still be so calm?" Wang Xiaojian looked at Qiao Yi in surprise.

"In the past few months, I have been mostly busy in the studio and seldom surfed the Internet. I haven't had time to watch the new product advertisement. Please don't get me wrong. In fact,

I am very happy that my work can bring positive effects to your company. But...you call me Beauty Qiao again, then I'll call you Brilliance Wang~" Qiao Yi was a little relaxed, as well as her voice seemed softer.

"You call me Brilliance Wang, that's good. It sounds like we are brother and sister. You are wearing heeled shoes today, and your height is really close to my 180cm height." Wang Xiaojian's delicate face was filled with a big smile. Qiao Yi's skeleton is small and soft, with a figure of her early 172cm in good proportions and clean appearance, which naturally gives people a slim vision. Standing next to Bai Xuan, who is no less than 185cm tall, it's like a match made by heaven. Bai Xuan's close friend Zhu Linchuan was slightly shorter than Bai Xuan, but he was a good match of handsome men and beautiful women when he stood with Sun Chuheng.

"Brilliance Wang, what time do you plan to leave in the evening? Please don't forget to bring me with you and I take your ride." Previously, Bai Xuan told Wang Xiaojian not to leave in a hurry, so that he would not order takeaway for dinner when he returned home alone, then he and Qiao Yi stayed together.

"About 10 o'clock in the evening, I will drive the assistant's car. You, hee hee, will find out later." Wang Xiaojian said with a funny smile. At this time, the smart remote control in Qiao Yi's hand responded. It seemed that the two babies were about to wake up, so she went to the villa with Wang Xiaojian.

Aunt Li had just finished her work on the second floor, while Uncle Li was still working as a gardener. When in the afternoon, Bai Xuan told the dinner to be delayed a little. Wang Xiaojian had nothing to do. He played with Qiao Yi and the two children. He sat on the blanket and built up wooden games. Sometimes he pretended to be a vivid animal, and sometimes he twisted smart toys to make the two children laugh haha. The capable assistant turned into a big boy.

Qiao Yi thought that since the contract has been signed, she will do her best to perform the task of caring and teaching the two children in the future. She took the initiative to ask Aunt Li for her experience in raising children humbly, and Aunt Li happily gave the book "Children's Parenting Classic" explained by Bai Rou and Xiao Yin to Qiao Yi for safekeeping, comforting Qiao Yi like a mother: "Daughter Qiao, relax. Don't worry, these two babies are very easy to take care of. They eat, drink, play and sleep very regular almost every day, so you don't have to worry about them."

Uncle Li finally finished his work as a gardener, walked into the villa to rest for a while, and meticulously trimmed the flowers and trees in the garden with originality and a new look. Aunt Li looked at the clock and felt that it was almost time to start preparing dinner, so she pulled Uncle Li and walked into the kitchen. When Qiao Yi saw Wang Xiaojian helping to look after the babies, she sat on the side and continued to read the book "Children's Parenting Classic" carefully. After reading, Her inexperienced little white rabbit cultivated into a parenting master who seemed to have experienced a hundred battles.

"Oh, Aunt Li, Youyou and Xiuxiu are shitting. Come here!" Wang Xiaojian who was playing with the two babies suddenly cried out.

"I'm here. Please don't bother Aunt Li." Qiao Yi put down the book, put on sanitary clothes and gloves, then carried the two babies to the washroom. Aunt Li, who came out of the kitchen, saw that Qiao Yi had skillfully changed the diapers for the two babies, and couldn't help being a little surprised. Even Wang Xiaojian, who was next to her, opened his mouth and gave the thumbs up: "I can't believe you are learning and using it. Awesome!"

Next, Aunt Li happily brought over the nutritious porridge and minced meat vegetables at the right temperature to let Qiao Yi feed to the twins. As soon as the two little ones saw delicious food in the bowls and spoons, their big round eyes were brightly straight. They stared at Qiao Yi for an instant, grinning dancingly, revealing a few cute little deciduous teeth, and shouting excitedly "food, food".

After the two babies finished eating and playing for a while, Aunt Li took them into the bathroom to take a bubble bath. Qiao Yi also came in wearing sanitary clothes and gloves to help Aunt Li, but she didn't expect that the two little ones giggled and asked her to take a bath with them.

When it was dinner time, Bai Xuan only came down from the third floor. Wang Xiaojian helped Uncle Li and Aunt Li, arranging the dining area, while Qiao Yi put the two babies who had just finished bathing and dressing in the baby chair, and handed them milk bottles to drink.

Bai Xuan was free after dinner, then he called Uncle Li and Aunt Li to the second floor to chat privately, yet Wang Xiaojian and Qiao Yi were with the two babies.

Qiao Yi asked Wang Xiaojian pitifully: "How long do we have to stay at Mr. Bai's house? Can we leave?"

Wang Xiaojian: "You can't leave... Beauty Qiao, didn't you understand the contract signed this afternoon?"

Qiao Yi: "Contract? I read it closely, and I signed it carefully after reading it. About the contract date… What does this have to do with going home?"

Wang Xiaojian covered his face with hands, and couldn't bear to lie to Qiao Yi: "Your contract will take effect as soon as it arrives today. I won't tell you too much. You can get the contract and see it yourself again. In case the more I tell you, the more mistakes I make, then later I will be probably beaten by the boss."

After Bai Xuan with Uncle Li and Aunt Li finished talking, the three returned to the first floor, approaching Qiao Yi them.

It was Uncle Li who spoke first: "Then my wife and I will go back first." Bai Xuan nodded calmly: "Okay." At this time, Wang Xiaojian, who looked so smart, couldn't wait to say: "Boss, then I'll go back too."

Just as Qiao Yi wanted to go with Wang Xiaojian, she was stopped by Bai Xuan: "Qiao Yi, you stay."

"Huh?!!!" As if being hit by thunders, Qiao Yi instinctively wanted to refuse, making everyone else laugh.

Aunt Li approached Qiao Yi and patted her on the shoulder kindly: "Daughter Qiao, Mr. Bai will give us two elders a weekend to rest. I'll trouble you to take care of the two babies. Don't be nervous, if you have any question need us to help, you can talk to Uncle Li and me at any time."

Wang Xiaojian added fuel to it: "Yes, yes, if you need help, you can always contact me too. I'm the universal assistant."

"But I didn't bring anything. I didn't have a change of clothes or laundry supplies." Qiao Yi said embarrassedly.

"It's all ready in your room on the second floor. I'll show you later." Bai Xuan looked at Qiao Yi softly.

Seeing that she really couldn't leave anyway, Qiao Yi had to respond to Bai Xuan obediently: "Okay... I'll stay..."

Aunt Li and Uncle Li fondly touched the pretty faces of the two babies to say goodbye, and Wang Xiaojian also winked cheekily with Qiao Yi to imply "I'm leaving, Beauty Qiao~". Qiao Yi could only watch Uncle Li and Wang Xiaojian drive away respectively.

Only Bai Xuan, Qiao Yi and the two babies were left in the huge villa. Qiao Yi seemed to be able to hear her own heartbeat, so nervous that her mind went blank. She didn't know what to say, then she could only bend over to appease the playful twins.

"Qiao Yi?" "Huh?" "Are you afraid?" "Um..." "Don't be afraid. It's safe here."

Bai Xuan also bent down and looked at Qiao Yi affectionately, while Qiao Yi's face felt too hot to escape. She was thinking: Too bad... Can Bai Xuan please stop being charming... She is afraid that she is getting deeper and deeper feelings... Falling in love with Bai Xuan but can't afford to match with him... Difficult to extricate herself at end...

"Come here, I'll take you to the second floor and have a look your room." Bai Xuan stretched out his hand to hold Qiao Yi then hugged Youyou.

"Thank you." Qiao Yi looked at Bai Xuan with mixed feelings, hugged another baby Xiuxiu, and followed behind Bai Xuan.

It turned out that Aunt Li was busy on the second floor in the afternoon to furnish Qiao Yi with a suite facing the sea, a luxurious balcony, a luxurious bedroom, a luxurious bathroom, and a luxurious clothing room, all of which were newly bought. Qiao Yi seemed to be in a dream. This scene was many times more powerfully shocked than when Bai Xuan took her to the private garden club for dinner at the first time. She stared at Bai Xuan's alluring back and stunned. Listening to his magnetic voice introducing the suite to herself, a warm current rushed into her heart, making her not know how to express the grateful words.

The two babies were sleeping soundly on Qiao Yi's big bed. "How about you let Youyou and Xiuxiu sleep with me and don't put them back in the baby's room, okay?" Qiao Yi looked at Bai Xuan softly. "Okay, you also go to bed early. Good night..." "Good night..."

Bai Xuan then exited and closed the door for Qiao Yi. However, Qiao Yi exhaled slowly when she heard him quietly walk away from her suite. After bathing, Qiao Yi walked to the balcony by wearing a fitted silk pajamas, feeling the pleasant sea breeze blow on her face and the melody of the waves touch in her heart. She went back to the bed to lie down, kissed the two babies' foreheads, and fell asleep together.

Chapter Eleven: Birthdays

Most of Qiao Yi's activity trajectory is about the small studio and the small duplex flat, two-point in one-line. And now an additional point is that she has to live in the Baixuan's villa on weekends to take care of the two cute babies, which has become a three-point in one-line activity trajectory.

The new product advertisement of Bai Group has become very popular on the whole network platform. As well as the related technology products with the new robot pillow are sold all over the world, that the sales record has been continuously refreshed. At the company's regular meeting, Chen Yuanzhi was finally able to hold his head up high, he was about to become the new favorite of everyone, and the controversy that had been raging against him in the past was finally subdued.

Not only that, the new product advertisement also brought the artist who appeared on the scene to sing the song "Where the Dreams Are" created by Qiao Yi to become a popular superstar. His agency already contacted Chen Yuanzhi specifically, and asked him to contact Qiao Yi on his behalf, intending to buy more authorized songs to create a broader successful road for their own artists. When Qiao Yi received a call from Chen Yuanzhi, she heard that the agency was planning to bring the superstar and Qiao Yi to meet for a dinner. Qiao Yi quickly begged Chen Yuanzhi to help her to politely refuse. She was afraid of socializing and also afraid of being photographed by fans of the superstar then exposed and scribbled. After all, no matter how popular the song is, not many people will pay attention to who the composer is. Qiao Yi discussed with Chen Yuanzhi, for asking her apprentice Liu Qiulan to talk to the agency about authorizing more other songs. Chen Yuanzhi said that there should be no problem, and he would also personally come forward to negotiate the prices for her.

Before the Winter Solstice festival, it was the birthdays of Qiao Yi and the two cute babies. In previous years, Qiao Yi simply celebrated her birthday or not at all. This year is very different. Bai Xuan told Aunt Li to prepare the birthdays early, and also asked Uncle Li to drive Qiao Yi from the studio to the villa.

Sun Chuheng and Zhu Linchuan also happened to be free from their busy schedules of support work and called their friends respectively.

Qiao Yi: "Ah-Heng, how are you and Brother Zhu Linchuan? And Lamu? How are you all doing?"

Sun Chuheng: "Everyone is doing well, yet you are the only one to worry about. My dear girl, Lamu and his fellow villagers would like to thank you for purchasing purple jade to make sculptures to promote their hometown. Yesterday, when the members of the medical teams had a dinner together, I also met Lamu, and he asked me to say hello to you. Oh, let me gossip with you that Lamu is in love. And his love is a soft girl from the famous Jiangnan Water Town in a fertile land of the eastern region, named Liu Ruyan. It sounds good she met Lamu when she came here for teaching."

Qiao Yi: "Oops, when I ask your development with Brother Zhu Linchuan, you always like to gossip about Lamu. What about the two of you?"

Sun Chuheng: "It's still the same. There is no new development between Zhu Linchuan and me. He as a man with well-developed limbs, is simply a peacock with flowers.

Everywhere he goes, he attracts a lot of young girls to admire him, and I can't stand his narcissism and cheekiness. But how far have you gotten along with the tall, rich and handsome Bai Xuan of the Bai Group? I think he is interested in you~"

Qiao Yi: "Ah-Heng, please don't talk nonsense... and don't tempt me to fantasize... At best I'm just his nephew and niece's nanny... The gap between him and me is too big. It's almost impossible... An ordinary storage room in his villa is better and bigger than my whole small flat... I can't afford to match with him... Unlike you and Brother Zhu Linchuan, the two of you are evenly matched and very suitable!"

Sun Chuheng: "Hey, my silly girl, let's not talk about this. I'm calling you today mainly to wish you a happy birthday. Originally, I wanted to cook a big meal for you, but now I have to break my promise and wait until March next year. When I come back, then make up the unique meal for you~"

Qiao Yi: "Okay, when you come back from the western region triumphantly, it's my turn to cook you a big meal. Also, please help me to convey to Lamu, when will he marry his love? I'm going to send them a pair of dragon and phoenix purple jade carvings as gifts for their wedding by the time."

Sun Chuheng: "Don't worry, darling. I will help you to tell Lamu and Liu Ruyan. They will definitely be very happy for your gifts~"

Before the birthdays of Qiao Yi and the two cute babies, Bai Xuan handled all the work in the office properly, then specially took a small time to return to the villa home. At this moment, his phone rang that it was Zhu Linchuan who just called.

Bai Xuan: "Linchuan? What kind of wind brought you to me? And What kind of chatter do you want to talk about this time?"

Zhu Linchuan: "My buddy, I'm not thinking of you, I'm here to say happy birthday to my twins nephew and niece, and I'll make up the gifts when I come back in March. It's too much about fate, that Qiao Yi was also born on the same day. Chuheng was just talking with Qiao Yi next to me, but now she ignores me. So I can only come to you my brother, to comfort my injured little young heart! Hey, your company's new product advertisement "Where the Dreams Are" is very high quality, and it is very popular on the whole network, which is almost dominating all the screens~"

Bai Xuan: "Well, it's different from the route my second uncle took when he controlled of the Group. I can't be like him to play the good cards all in bad results."

Zhu Linchuan: "When your second uncle was in power, he was absolutely a plagiarism king. He made almost all the advertisements of the Bai Group look like they were selling sanitary napkins. When saw such vulgar and ugly advertisements on the big LED screen, at that time, I almost forgot that your company mainly promotes high-end technology and fashion products."

Bai Xuan: "I remember that before my grandfather died, my second uncle and second aunt were so opposed to me coming back home after I finished my studies abroad, because they wanted to illegally swallow the Bai Group into their own pockets. However, they have the guts but no brains, as well as short-sighted."

Zhu Linchuan: "Speaking of your second aunt, when I was investigating the local vaccine accident in the western areas this time, I found that she had an indirect relationship with the local suspect, and not only that, she also involved in gene trafficking cases, using the cooperative intermediaries selling the people's genetic data to foreign secret agencies. The National Security Center has taken over this matter. It is best for you to let the lawyer department and the public relation department of Bai Group cooperate well, then follow the clues to ensure that you are not involved. If you need help, My parents them should still be able to help you. Although they have retired from the Disciplinary Inspection Commission, they still have some friendship there, and they will handle it fairly to minimize your losses."

Bai Xuan: "Linchuan, thank you for reminding me. I have made arrangements for these matters, and I will investigate them secretly and carefully."

Zhu Linchuan: "About your younger cousin, I heard from my elder cousin that he seems to have something to do with the underworld forces in Oceania. Do you remember my elder cousin? The one who is resident in the country's overseas base, married a local girl as his wife, and settled down there."

Bai Xuan: "Yes, I remember. Your elder cousin once pursued my elder cousin, but unfortunately my elder cousin had no intention of it. Later, she married a top science and technology professor from the Western European island country and gave birth to a pair of mixed-race twin daughters. Now the whole family lives in the northern capital of the country. The husband and the wife both are teaching at the Centennial National University and at the same time working in the affiliated aviation research base."

Zhu Linchuan: "Oh, we played together in the military compound when we were young. Your second aunt can't see your elder cousin who was born by your second uncle's late ex-wife, then they threw her to your grandfather's house. But your younger cousin never played with us, never closed to us, and has been spoiled by your second uncle and second aunt since childhood."

Bai Xuan: "He has become like this now. It is estimated that my second aunt spread the bad gene from the mother's womb to her son."

After Bai Xuan and Zhu Linchuan ended the call, he rubbed his temples and linked the second uncle, the second aunt and the younger cousin, their whole family behind his back done secret activities over the years, one by one, the picture emerged. It seems that they have already rotted from the root.

Qiao Yi brought two pair of sterling silver bell bracelets as gifts for the dragon-phoenix twins. She was going to put them on for the dragon-phoenix twins at the birthday banquet in the evening. At the moment, she was playing with the pair of one-year-old twins on the smooth and fresh lawn in the garden. Standing on the balcony with the best view from the third floor, Bai Xuan stared at Qiao Yi and the twins playing happily on the lawn, and the corners of his mouth curled into a smile.

The warm birthday banquet began, where the exquisite cakes shone with colorful brilliance. Uncle Li and Aunt Li specially cooked delicious longevity noodles for Qiao Yi, and also prepared traditional fiery eggs for the first-year-old two adorable babies. The highlight moment of sortition is approaching. Surrounding the dragon-phoenix twins are the dazzling arrays of meaningful gifts, but it is very strange, the two babies are staring at Qiao Yi's sterling silver bell bracelets, babbling mischievously, picking up the bell bracelets and thinking about to put them on their chubby little hands and feet. Qiao Yi was very happy. She quickly stepped forward gently to help the two babies wear the silver bracelets with the crisp sound of bells. The two babies seemed to be full of joy, their little hands were clinging to Qiao Yi's wrist, their round and lovely big eyes were shining with stars, and they were vaguely calling Qiao Yi "Mom, Mom~". Their cute little milky voices amused Uncle Li and Aunt Li to laugh joyfully.

Bai Xuan raised his eyebrows slightly. He was a little surprised that his one-year-old nephew and niece were so attached to Qiao Yi, even picking gifts from Qiao Yi, and calling Qiao Yi "mom" indiscriminately. It was late bedtime after the birthday banquet. Uncle Li and Aunt Li saw that the two babies were going to sleep on the bed in Qiao Yi's room again, so they relaxed and prepared to rest.

After taking a bath, Qiao Yi cleaned up a little bit, then planned to lie down on the bed and sleep with the two babies in a sweet dream. When the door rang, Qiao Yi thought that Aunt Li was looking for her for something, and hurriedly stepped forward to open the door, but what caught her eye was Bai Xuan who had just taken a bath. Qiao Yi couldn't help blushing at the tips of her ears, her face was a little dazed, and she was muttering in her heart: What a perfect person... He looks so handsome even in home clothes... Under the dark and high-cold home clothes, there is still a vague and icy temperament...

Bai Xuan seriously took out a large gift box from behind and handed it to Qiao Yi: "Here is for you, the custom-made dress, shoes and necklace, as your 23rd birthday gift, and please put them on tomorrow. Can you have time now to chat with me on the balcony outside for a while?"

"Okay, I'll see how Youyou and Xiuxiu are sleeping, then come right away." When Bai Xuan turned to the balcony, Qiao Yi suddenly read a single trace of sadness from his back... After seeing the two babies were already fast asleep, Qiao Yi followed Bai Xuan.

"Thank you for your gift. It's gorgeous. But I didn't give anything for your birthday last month." Qiao Yi was somewhat ashamed.

"It's all right. You sent a message to congratulate me, not to mention that the hotel I stayed in during my business trip has hosted a birthday banquet for me. I asked you to come out, yet talk so late. Is it cold?" Bai Xuan reached out and touched Qiao Yi's delicate oval face.

"It's not cold. Look at how beautiful the starry sky is tonight. The deep sea under the brilliance is very unique. Even the lights of the thousands of homes around you are shining like pearls." Qiao Yi felt Bai Xuan's emotions and tried to make him happy.

"Well, you are also very beautiful." Bai Xuan stared at Qiao Yi from the affection of his eyes, then turned to face Qiao Yi and said, "Our Bai Group intends to promote an advertising short film focusing on fashion products in the spring of next year. In the conception stage, there is no public bidding yet. Are you interested in creating the promotional song and background story plan? You must submit the manuscript before the Lunar New Year."

Qiao Yi vaguely heard Bai Xuan said that she was in beauty making her heart beat like a deer dancing, then instantly heard that Bai Xuan gave her the opportunity to be in charge of the new promotion song for the next short commercial film of Bai Group. "Huh?" Her eyes lit up, "Yes, I am interested!"

"Okay, after the Winter Solstice festival, you can come to my office and have a detailed talk with Manager Chen." Bai Xuan said in a light voice.

"No problem! Thank you very much for giving me another chance. I will work hard to complete a good creation." Qiao Yi's eyes lit up with the starry shine.

Bai Xuan fixedly looked at Qiao Yi and sensed that her body exuded the innate cleanness and agility, which made people feel comfortable naturally. Bai Xuan changed the topic: "Do you think it is strange that you have never seen messages from the parents of the dragon-phoenix twins?"

Qiao Yi did have doubts in her heart, but she didn't think much for Bai Xuan's special family background being different from ordinary people. However, at this time, Bai Xuan suddenly asked this question, which made her feel somewhat worried: "Yes... Did something happen...?"

Bai Xuan moved his lips slightly, while his voice was fairly low: "Yes, the parents of the dragon-phoenix twins have passed away, and they will be raised by me in the future."

Qiao Yi found it hard to accept the news, as well as felt very sad for the pair of twins who had just turned one year old. They lost their biological parents at such a young age. Qiao Yi said

in a softly trembling voice: "They passed away... so suddenly...
I'm sorry... My condolences to the loss... "

Bai Xuan could see that Qiao Yi felt the same way and wanted
to comfort him: "My sister and my brother-in-law handed over
their two babies to me. I must have known in advance that an
accident would happen. The "In Vitro Fertility" genetic project
they are responsible for has already matured technology, and
the dragon-phoenix twins are one of the products. Life no
longer depends on the birth of a female womb. In order to
prevent their scientific research results from falling into the
international institutions manipulated by other major countries
for a large number of illegal profits, the two authorized all the
patents of "In Vitro Fertility" genetic project to our country.
Later, the international institutions manipulated by other major
countries sent major representatives. When they came to the
research base shared by my sister and my brother-in-law,
unfortunately, a conflict between the two sides caused an
unknown explosion. The site was destroyed in all dead."

Qiao Yi marveled that Youyou and Xiuxiu came from the "In
Vitro Fertility" technology, which was completely beyond her
current understanding. "Then... do you know who the
murderers are? Your sister and you brother-in-law are so top-
notch, who are rare international scientists."

"The direct murderers are dead. Even if the real murderers are
known, it will not be disclosed to the public. To snatch high-
end technology and elite talents, which has always been a cruel
competition among world powers, so many dark sides cannot
be known to the public. Rest assured, the news of this matter
will be broadcast soon, it has been muffled for some time, and
our country has now cleaned up the tail."

Qiao Yi got the courage from her instinctive reaction. When she heard Bai Xuan finish the words, she moved her hand to touch Bai Xuan's fingertips to give him warm support: "I will do my duty to take care of Youyou and Xiuxiu." Bai Xuan raised a relieved smile, and he was gently approaching her.

The next morning, Qiao Yi and Aunt Li were busy together. It turned out that Qiao Yi, with Bai Xuan's consent, was concentrating on packing all kinds of exquisite foods and gifts to bring to the two apprentices in the studio and the old cleaning aunt and the old security man of the building.

Uncle Li drove the car out of the garage, together with Qiao Yi, put the packed gift boxes in the back compartment and fixed them. They said goodbye to the two babies in the stroller pushed by Aunt Li, then waited for Bai Xuan to come down from the third floor... A new day begins, the sun is shining, the sea is blue, as well as the sky is clear. The flowers and trees are still lush, yet the fearless Winter Solstice is coming.

Chapter Twelve: Lunar New Year

Authoritative media publicly reported that Bai Rou and Xiao Yin, an ethnic Chinese couple who died unfortunately some time ago, are internationally recognized outstanding scientists, successful in the mature technology of "In Vitro Fertility" genetic project, bringing good news for heterosexuals, homosexuals and even singles to continue their offspring according to their own wishes, that the birth of life can be freed from the restrictions of female womb and traditional gestation. The public was in an uproar, and there was a lot of heated discussion in private. They were surprised that nowadays science and technology have quietly progressed so much.

If the people who are popcorn-munching masses have a little more leisure time, they will search for gossip everywhere. They noticed that the former acting boss of the Bai Group with his whole family has lived in Oceania for a long time after the retirement. Just not long ago, their only son was killed in a gang fight. The old couple is heartbroken.

Bai Xuan stood like a static statue in his private office, the expression between his eyebrows was as cold as a sword, the air around him seemed to freeze into ice, he said nothing, and his eyes were bottomless. The high-end, expensive, limited-edition mobile phone lay flat on the desk in loneliness. Even if it rang many times then stopped, its owner seemed disdainful of answering the incoming calls.

When the incoming call was annoying again, Bai Xuan faintly stretched out his long fingers and pressed the answer button. "Bai Xuan! You must die brutally!! You framed my son! One day you will be bombed to pieces like your sister and your brother-in-law!!" On the other end of the phone came the message from an aggressive and insidious middle-aged woman, with a hoarse and twisted voice, swearing viciously and furiously.

"Oh? My second aunt, didn't yourself kill your precious son? Ask your heart how many bad things your whole family has done over the years?! This time, Interpol is to eliminate harm for the people and eradicate those major gangs and underworlds who have been entrenched for a long time. You should be thankful, so that you and my second uncle can live more at ease in Oceania. Why do you have the leisure to curse me?" Bai Xuan's words were as indifferent as frost. He is like a cold-blooded viper attacking the enemy.

"Humph! Do you think that if you grab the president power from your second uncle and even drive us all out of the Bai Group, you will be able to secure your position? You are dreaming!" The middle-aged woman screamed like a red monster, "I will curse you to death!"

"Your husband used to be the acting boss of the Bai Group, didn't he step on the bloody corpses of my parents who died early?! If you could bring me down, I'm afraid I would have died seven or eight hundred times!" Bai Xuan's cold air is threatening the other.

After hanging up the phone, Bai Xuan put the mobile phone aside and fell into deep thought. His second uncle is as rotten as mud, that it is difficult to attach to the wall. He has made Bai Group a mess for so many years. It is his painstaking efforts to bring the Group back to life, but his second aunt has always been ruthless. She kept to put her own eyeliners in the Group, and wished she would use all means to get rid of him, so that her arrogant and domineering baby son would come back to control the throne of the president. Now that her son has died suddenly, she was disillusioned, then she planed to destroy Bai Xuan too.

According to the strict requirements of Bai Group, Qiao Yi finally completed the short film script and promotion song "Colors" for fashion products in time before the Lunar New Year. The style of the song is soul-stirring and unique, and it is very different from the previous song "Where the Dreams are", which promoted technology products. Chen Yuanzhi warmly informed Qiao Yi to come to the Bai Group building to sign the relevant authorization contract.

When the authorization contract was placed in front of Qiao Yi, she was quite confused: how come there are several more zeros in the payment amount this time?? The first promotion song for technology products was already a very high payment price, which was shocking to her as a newcomer!!

"Manager Chen, is such a large payment amount wrong?" Qiao Yi asked Chen Yuanzhi earnestly and frankly.

"Is there? I'll check again." Chen Yuanzhi took the contract with both hands, and squinted his wise eyes to read the black words on the white papers carefully.

A while later, Qiao Yi heard Chen Yuanzhi's cheerful voice with the smile: "Don't worry, the payment amount is correct. Your work is worthy of such a high payment amount. Actually our Group evaluates it based on the market value brought by your work."

After signing the authorization contract, Chen Yuanzhi gave Qiao Yi a brief introduction about Bai Group's huge production bases of technology products and fashion products, as well as real estate assets such as high-end commercial malls and hotels at home and abroad. So that, the payment amount of her works does not seem to be anything, although it is already astronomical for her, who belongs to the ordinary people.

Chen Yuanzhi mentioned that his wife and children liked the poetry collections written by Qiao Yi, especially the story poems series. He accordingly took out the full version which he bought from the bookstore and asked for Qiao Yi helping to sign it. Qiao Yi was very surprised and delighted. She has always been like treating her own works as her own children.

She hurriedly thanked Chen Yuanzhi, picked up the book, wrote blessings and signed her signature.

When Chen Yuanzhi and Qiao Yi were talking about the topic of the Lunar New Year, Wang Xiaojian happened to open the glass door of the reception room and walked in, shouting: "The boss has just finished a meeting with the secretary department, then he has to discuss related matters with the lawyer department, so he can't come here. He told me to come down and take care of Qiao Yi, Beauty Qiao~" Qiao Yi knew Wang Xiaojian well that he was with a smart mouth, while she could only respond with a soft smile.

Chen Yuanzhi: "It just happened that my wife and children planned to go back to Qiongdao Island and Taidao Island to visit our in-laws during the Lunar New Year holiday. Xiao Wang, you are here. Come and sit down and talk. Qiao Yi, do you also plan to go back to your hometown to accompany your parents and relatives?"

Qiao Yi: "My parents are no longer alive, and there are no other close relatives in my hometown to visit. I think about to stay in Haicheng City for the Lunar New Year."

Wang Xiaojian had secretly investigated the detailed files of Qiao Yi in response to the private task given by Bai Xuan before. He knew that Qiao Yi was equivalent to an orphan, but his professional quality was strong enough and his face was thick enough too. At this moment, he could pretend to be knowing-nothing. His innocent eyes and delicate face showed the same deep sympathy as Chen Yuanzhi. Hearing that Chen Yuanzhi wanted to invite Qiao Yi with his family to go to the islands for the Lunar New Year, he hurriedly interjected with a smart smile: "Brother Chen, even if your family likes Qiao Yi a lot, it's not fair that you monopolize all the love. I guess I will have to go back to my hometown alone to celebrate the Lunar New Year, and when I meet my parents and relatives, I will be in the blind date meetings arranged by the aunts and uncles in turn. How about letting Qiao Yi pretend to be my girlfriend and go with me for the Lunar New Year holiday?"

Qiao Yi couldn't be calm: "I decide to stay in Haicheng City. Thank you for your all kindness." She is an indoor girl with a tendency to social fear, and she can't imagine how she can go to Wang Xiaojian's hometown. Maybe she would be surrounded by a large group of people looking at her as well as asking her with a lot of questions.

Chen Yuanzhi, Wang Xiaojian and Qiao Yi happily opened the chat mode, and they said goodbye to each other after a long while. But Wang Xiaojian insisted that it was Bai Xuan who asked him to drive Qiao Yi home in person, then in the end Qiao Yi had to give up taking the subway.

In the car, Qiao Yi really wanted to close her eyes for a rest, but she was always haunted by the talkative Wang Xiaojian: "Beauty Qiao, this time you have to help me free from single, and put those beauties around you who are also in the difficult situation of being single to introduce to me."

Qiao Yi listened to Wang Xiaojian's nagging like a grudge woman, while suddenly remembered that Lamu's fiancee Liu Ruyan mentioned in WeChat that her college friend had no experience of love and was looking for her Mr. Right too...

"There is a girl who is also single. She is an excellent teacher. How about you both add WeChat to each other then communicate privately, okay?"

"Thank you, as expected, Beauty Qiao's friends are all high-quality. Although this girl's appearance is not as good as yours, it meets my requirements~"

Wang Xiaojian was so happy as if he had won the jackpot with a big smile on his face, and it influenced Qiao Yi's heart that she was also happy to be a one-time matchmaker.

The Lunar New Year is getting closer. Qiao Yi thought that it was difficult for the two apprentices to get long-distance high-speed train tickets home during the peak time of the Spring Festival, so she bought plane tickets for Li Chunshu and Liu Qiulan respectively. The studio's first-year performance has made a good start, and it is the positive result of the team's joint efforts, so the bonuses of employees have become better with the performance. When Li Chunshu and Liu Qiulan received the generous year-end bonus that Qiao Yi gave them, they delighted gratefully with their mellow smiles that they were following the right boss, and both sincerely thanked Qiao Yi: "Master, you are so kind to us! Next year we will work harder to move forward!"

After the studio finished the last batch of engraving orders, with Li Chunshu and Liu Qiulan already coming back to their hometowns for the Lunar New Year, Qiao Yi stayed in her small home all day alone, writing poetry and music when she had thoughts, or reading books and playing songs on the electronic organ. Seeing every household is busy buying the Lunar New Year's goods, Qiao Yi was very simple, and only hanged the word "Fortune" on the family portrait of the three of them carved in wood.

Sun Chuheng and Zhu Linchuan made a video call to Qiao Yi. They were both in the western support area for the Lunar New

Year. Some time ago, they were still working on coordinating the use of various folk herbal medicines. With the assistance of Lamu and Liu Ruyan, the compilation of the entire herbal compendium was smoothly under way. It went well. The four of them took advantage of the holiday to relax, and they all went to Lamu's village hometown to celebrate the Lunar New Year. At this time, the group was roasting sweet potatoes by the earth stove. The flames were so strong that the faces of the four of them were about to reflect the red flowers. It was very lively, it seemed that the spraying sweet potato fragrance could be smelled through the screen of the mobile phone, and Qiao Yi was feeling so hungry to swallow saliva quietly.

After finishing the video call, Qiao Yi swiftly pulled out the purple potatoes prepared earlier from the food cabinet, followed the cooking skills that Aunt Li had taught, and began to cut the purple potatoes into small cubes. Then put them into the mini pot, and add an appropriate amount sugar, boiling with water. During the waiting process, Qiao Yi suddenly missed Uncle Li, Aunt Li and the twins. The old couple was heartbroken for a long time because of the death of the twins' parents, Bai Rou and Xiao Yin. From then on, they treated the twins as their grandchildren. But because of the troubles from Bai Xuan's second uncle's family, they were increasingly worried about Bai Xuan for his silent and cold appearance.

When the purple potato soup was about to come out of the pot, the doorbell rang. After Qiao Yi cleaned up the surroundings, she muttered to herself that ordinarily no one would visit her, so she was very cautious and curious to see who was outside through the peephole camera on the security door.

It's okay not to see it, but it's a great shock after seeing it! Qiao Yi got into the big stun as if she was suddenly hit by the grand prize given by God!

"Why did Bai Xuan suddenly appear at my door? Was it Wang Xiaojian making a snitch?" Qiao Yi took a deep breath then went to open the door.

When the eyesights of the two met, Qiao Yi pressed the tension and said first: "Mr. Bai??"

Bai Xuan leaned over and coughed lightly, with a magnetic and elegant voice: "Qiao Yi, can I come in and have a sit at your home?"

Qiao Yi answered with somewhat absent-mindedness: "Ah? Can... yes, of course, please... please come in."

After entering the house, Bai Xuan silently looked at Qiao Yi's mini duplex flat. The space is indeed very small, but the decoration style is ingenious and green. The open kitchen is connected to the small living room. Outside the floor-to-ceiling window is a chic small balcony. The attic is a semi-open small study and a small bedroom next to each other. Everything is taken care in an orderly manner.

The purple potato soup made by herself before was ready to serve, and when she was hungry, Qiao Yi asked Bai Xuan whether he wanted to try it too. After Bai Xuan nodded with a smile, she set the tableware for the two of them on the small dining table with the fragrant purple potato soup. Although Qiao Yi often couldn't help being shy when she met Bai Xuan, the two had the same tacit understanding.

"I heard from Xiao Wang about your situation. You can come with me later and celebrate the Lunar New Year together." Bai Xuan did not explicitly say that he had asked Wang Xiaojian to check Qiao Yi's detailed information files, while his eyes fell to the center of the closet. There was the family portrait of the three in wood carvings about a foot high, which were carefully carved by Qiao Yi alone on the back balcony of the building opposite his private office...

"Ah? Mr. Bai, you already know that I have no parents and no close relatives... But will it be troublesome for you if I go to your house for the Lunar New Year? Actually, I can celebrate the Lunar New Year by myself. I haven't done it alone before, but now I am able to..." Qiao Y said softly.

"Not troublesome, it's just Uncle Li, Aunt Li and the twins Youyou and Xiuxiu. They all miss you." Bai Xuan understood that Qiao Yi was afraid of causing inconvenience to him.

The two chatted while eating. Bai Xuan continued: "Purple potato soup is good, can I come to your house for a meal occasionally in the future?"

Qiao Yi frowned slightly, but answered without thinking too much: "Okay, if you don't mind my simple and small home, you are welcome at any time."

In this way, Bai Xuan persuaded Qiao Yi to his villa to celebrate the Lunar New Year together. Uncle Li and Aunt Li also knew about Qiao Yi's family background from Bai Xuan, so they naturally loved Qiao Yi as their daughter. The twins are now able to walk on their own. They are more cute and adorable, that they like to be sticky all the time with Qiao Yi and feel the gentle maternal aura from her.

During the Lunar New Year's Eve dinner, the six of them, old and young, sat around the revolving table enjoying the meal together, who were more like a family. The atmosphere was harmonious and warm.

Bai Xuan said to Qiao Yi gently, "Don't be cautious, and you don't need to use honorifics to me in the future, you can call me by my name."

Uncle Li and Aunt Li ruddied radiantly, smiled and agreed: "Daughter Qiao, you and us are like family. Please make yourself at home."

Qiao Yi was touched and unexpectedly able to integrate into Bai Xuan's family: "Thank you very much. I like you all, especially Youyou and Xiuxiu."

Originally, after dinner, everyone came to watch the Spring Festival Gala of the Lunar New Year show in the super spacious and fancy film and television hall, where the supplies for sitting on the floor, including the bed function, have been prepared. However, Uncle Li and Aunt Li may be old, they don't get used to tossing like young people. After watching the show for a while, their tired eyes were too sleepy. So the two elders simply went back to their room to rest.

In the huge and splendid film and television hall, this pair of dragon-phoenix twins babbled excitedly beside Qiao Yi and Bai Xuan, and intellectual toys were spread all over the floor. The two little ones are very good and regular. They fall asleep gradually at the corresponding time. Qiao Yi and Bai Xuan adjusted the smart lights in the entire hall to the soft color suitable for them sleeping. When the Lunar New Year moment was arriving, Qiao Yi also had lay down and fell asleep unconsciously, with a calm and peaceful breath. While seeing all that, Bai Xuan was greatly fascinated by her.

Time passed lightly in the night. Bai Xuan heard from the sleeping Qiao Yi with intermittent dream-words: Dad... Mom... Don't leave... Don't leave... He concernedly came to Qiao Yi to lie down, hugged her into his warm arms and patted her delicate back very affectionately to comfort her: Don't be afraid... You have me... You are not alone... I won't leave you... Perhaps feeling Bai Xuan's tenderness, Qiao Yi struggled for a while then returned to calm as well as fell into a deep sleep. Bai Xuan hugged Qiao Yi like this, and he seemed to hear the soft wind blowing outside the villa and the gentle waves swimming slowly in the beautiful late night.

Chapter Thirteen: To be Together

March in the western region, all things are revived and spring is full of blossoms. The support work of Sun Chuheng and Zhu Linchuan has already come to an end, which has greatly improved the quality of the medical teams, the supervision and inspection system and the urban and rural health education work in the whole county of Yucheng City. At the same time, their project was approved by the state for the development of local people's livelihood to build an advanced comprehensive Chinese herbal medicine base.

With the development of the large-scale pharmaceutical factory project, Sun Chuheng and Zhu Linchuan, as the head of the project and one of the main shareholders, the plan to return to Haicheng City was postponed to June accordingly. Because of the love for this land after getting along for more than half a year, Yucheng City has long been regarded as Sun Chuheng and Zhu Linchuan's second home.

As for Qiao Yi, her studio's orders are overwhelmingly busy to handle. Li Chunshu and Liu Qiulan have been carefully cultivated by Qiao Yi. Now they are quite good at the different carvings of normal difficulty level. They can already be on their own and become the right and left hands of Qiao Yi.

As for Bai Xuan, he focused on optimizing the work within the Group. Many of his second uncle or second aunt's eyeliners were eliminated. The entire Group's decision-making level willingly obeyed Bai Xuan's leadership, and even competitors had to admire his talent.

In the quaint and elegant private garden club of the wealthy area, all high-quality staffs appeared in front of Bai Xuan and reported the information to him who was sitting on the high chair: "Boss, the matter over Oceania has been dealt with. It's completed." Bai Xuan tapped the sandalwood table with his fingertips, and replied calmly: "You all did a good job, and you all step back first."

No one could have imagined that these service staffs employed in the garden club were actually an elite team of detectives belonging to Bai Xuan, whose intelligence work could spread across all continents. Bai Xuan sat quietly, waiting for something in no hurry.

The phone rang, while the angry hoarse middle-aged woman's voice came from the receiver: "Good trick! Bai Xuan, no matter how ruthless I am, I can't compare to your one-and-a-half move! Anyway, I have nowhere to go now, and I am a dying person! Don't expect I will be afraid of you! Even though you know the secrets of what happened back then, I have already done all the bad things!"

Bai Xuan sat on the high chair, his long legs changed the posture leisurely. When he spat out every single word from his seductive lips, he shot at his second aunt like the cold arrow: "I have nothing more to say. You aim to ruin my everything but you can't be crazy any more. You, go to hell!"

The middle-aged woman over the phone was too panic to speak, yet a middle-aged man next to her grabbed the microphone and hurriedly said to Bai Xuan: "Xuan'er, it's us, your second uncle and second aunt's fault. I'm here to apologize to you. You see me and your second aunt have deserved the retribution. Your younger cousin died tragically in the underworld's gang fight. We white-haired people held the black-haired person's funeral. Even your elder cousin didn't recognize me as a father... Back then, when I was confused for that moment, I conspired with your second aunt to kill your parents, deceptively seized the controlling stake in the Group, but later almost destroyed the foundation established by our ancestors. No matter what we do now, we can't make up for the mistakes we made. The Group shares and the property transferred under your name is all the compensation that I can give to you. I have already handed over the transfer procedures, please also tell your elder cousin on my behalf..."

After Bai Xuan heard his second uncle's words, he still didn't have much emotion, and described the facts coldly: "Back then you poisoned my parents to win the Group, pretending that they killed each other suddenly. If it wasn't for the housekeeper secretly asked Uncle Li and Aunt Li to send me and Bai Rou to Grandpa's place, I guess we would have already died under your hands! In order to save the entire Group and prevent the turmoil, Grandpa also sent the housekeeper with his whole family to work and live overseas, and gave out a large amount of property and money to the housekeeper to make him worry-free. I learned the truth before the housekeeper died. Besides, Bai Group did not belong to you in the first place. You and your wife cruelly and unscrupulously occupied it, as well as absurdly plotted the Group to be inherited by your dead evil son in the future. Go ahead your daydreams! Even if I don't count the fact that you poisoned my parents, you, your wife and your son have committed a lot of crimes that can be sentenced to death! I don't think I'm a good person, but I did a justice business this time. About my elder cousin, she doesn't recognize you as father, I also agree. About your property, since you transferred it to me, I will donate it, giving to the national poverty alleviation institution that can be considered as doing some public welfare."

After Bai Xuan's second uncle and second aunt heard the last call, they both fell to the ground like the exhausted old leather balls.

As the days go by, People pay attention to the gossip news of the Bai Group. Occasionally, there are sporadic reports that the former acting boss of the Bai Group and his wife both died in Oceania not long ago. They set off a fire at home and committed suicide.

Sun Chuheng and Zhu Linchuan have begun to expand in the busy large pharmaceutical factory base in the western region. In order to celebrate this event, everyone happily discussed holding a lively dinner party and carefully selected the event venue for the dinner party.

In the early summer of June, Yucheng City, where is backed by the mountains in the western region, is not as hot and sticky as Haicheng City, where is near the sea in the southern region. The air is full of fresh, natural, cool and pleasant. The motherland is so vast, and the four seasons are so different from the South to the North and from the West to the East.

Accompanied by Lamu and Liu Ruyan, Sun Chuheng and Zhu Linchuan walked and stopped in the suburbs of Yucheng City, looking at the beautiful scenery of the city and countryside bathed in green mountains and clean water from a distance, which suddenly gave people an endless sense of joy.

Zhu Linchuan put away his jubilant temperament and said to Sun Chuheng in a rare and serious manner: "Chuheng, I plan to buy a piece of land and build a villa-style house here. Together we will plant flower garden, vegetable farm, and herb field. Do you agree?"

Sun Chuheng thought he was joking, but looking at the firmness in his eyes, she replied affectionately and decisively: "Agree."

At the dinner party, most of them were positive and energetic young people. Many girls admired the handsome and bright Zhu Linchuan, so often ran up to talk to him, causing him to explain in a hurry that he had a future wife already. Sun Chuheng saw his slightly comical performance, she smiled then turned to the large garden outside the dinner venue to breathe the fresh air. Lamu and Liu Ruyan sat opposite Zhu Linchuan yet blinked fiercely, implying that he need to hurry up to chase after Sun Chuheng.

Zhu Linchuan ran out with a little drunk to look for Sun Chuheng's beautiful figure, but was surprised to see two refined boys in front discussing who should go first to express love to Sister Chuheng, which aroused Zhu Linchuan's great jealousy, and came quickly in hurry steps. He said loudly in front of the two boys: "Stop! That's my future wife. Your two guys want to get a thrashing?!"

The two refined boys were frightened, they cutely made a foolish apology then ran away, worried that Zhu Linchuan would catch up and ask for a fight.

Standing on the edge of the garden, Sun Chuheng watched Zhu Linchuan use such childish behavior to frighten off the two refined boys, while her eyes were even more tender. They get along with each other day and night, and they have long been tacit understanding of each other's hearts without words.

Zhu Linchuan approached Sun Chuheng like a big loyal dog wagging its tail, stretched out his arms and hugged her tightly: "Chuheng, marry me."

At this moment, Sun Chuheng was snuggling into Zhu Linchuan's hot arms like a little girl, whispering on his lips: "Well, we're getting married."

Two months later, it was reported that Lamu and Liu Ruyan, Zhu Linchuan and Sun Chuheng registered their marriage at the Civil Affairs Bureau on the same day.

Qiao Yi was shut to the outside world, until Sun Chuheng graciously showed her and Zhu Linchuan's marriage certificate in front of her, then Qiao Yi suddenly widened her eyes and looked up and down over joyfully at her close friend whom she hadn't seen for quite a long time.

Sun Chuheng patted Qiao Yi's head dotingly: "Ah-Yi, my girl, I already registered marriage. The wedding party is scheduled for mid-August. It happens that my birthday is in early August, and Linchuan's birthday is in late August, so the August is really becoming our lucky month. You also need to catch up, and don't let the single diamond king Bai Xuan run away. I'm still waiting to see you get married, haha~"

Qiao Yi looked at the bright red marriage certificate curiously, and happily leaned on Sun Chuheng: "Don't make fun of me. It's a surprise that you quietly got married on the same day as Lamu and Liu Ruyan. My Sister Ah-Heng and Brother Zhu Linchuan are finally the blessed couple. For the wedding ceremony, I wish you two give an early birth of lovely kids. I will reset the gifts. Before I was going to send the dragon and phoenix purple jade carvings to Lamu and Liu Ruyan. Now I can't make another pair in time. I will change to give two sets of Dragon and Phoenix Jewelry for you two couples."

Sun Chuheng waved her hand: "Ah, Linchuan and I both like whatever Ah-Yi give to us, and I believe Lamu and Liu Ruyan do too."

Qiao Yi smiled sweetly, her voice soft and waxy: "Is it ok I won't be a bridesmaid at your wedding?"

Sun Chuheng knew that Qiao Yi was introverted and not used to being in contact with many people, so she hugged her soft shoulders carefully: "Don't worry. I know you are afraid of the vast people. I will let your two apprentices Li Chunshu and Liu Qiulan do this. You are my girl, and I understand you."

The wedding came as scheduled. Among the three pairs of groomsmen and bridesmaids, one pair was Sun Chuheng and Zhu Linchuan's colleagues, one pair was Li Chunshu and Liu Qiulan, and the remaining pair was Wang Xiaojian and Liu Ruyan's good college friend. That girl is from the northern region, as a teacher with elegant and generous personality. During the time, she got to chat well with Wang Xiaojian.

Qiao Yi sat in an inconspicuous seat, watching the parents and relatives of the bride and groom gather together, and seeing the kindness of Sun Chuheng's family when they handed over their daughter to Zhu Linchuan, she was very touched, as well as quietly wiped the tears from the corners of her eyes.

Perhaps she looked at the bride and groom too concentrated. Qiao Yi didn't notice that Bai Xuan had switched seats and came to sit next to her to watch her.

The arrival of September is the harvest season. After marriage, Sun Chuheng and Zhu Linchuan often travel back and forth between the western region and the southern region. The comprehensive pharmaceutical factory are opened up very successfully, thanks to the dedication of the two and the efforts of the professional team.

Qiao Yi's fashion product short film "Colors" for Bai Group was not only highly sought after on the Internet, but also unexpectedly won the gold award in the international short film group. Chen Yuanzhi was shocked, and even Bai Xuan was also surprised.

In addition, Qiao Yi also participated in the National Sculpture Competition in a low-key manner. Her "Western Picture Scroll" and "Dragon and Phoenix", which were meticulously carved by purple jade, won the special prize and the first prize respectively. When the awards were presented, Qiao Yi asked her two apprentices to accept the awards on her behalf. Watching the lights on the platform gather on Li Chunshu and Liu Qiulan, Qiao Yi, who was outside the Vanity Fair, smiled warmly.

The sharp-eyed netizens couldn't sit still, when they found that their favorite poetry collections, the sculptures they were rushing to collect, and the musics that they clicked crazily, yet the creator behind all these was actually the same person, named Qiao Yi. They ran to Qiao Yi's studio website to search, as well as spontaneously recommended it to the people around them. With such a passive reputation, Qiao Yi has received cooperation from many companies, and they would also intend to turn her works into films, dramas or musicals.

Qiao Yi felt very embarrassed that the netizens searched her like the star-chasing fans. Especially when someone took photos of her daily life by chance, they were shocked to find that she was more stunning than a star model, with the pure temperament and abstinence, and they even inexplicably felt that they earned a lot for being Qiao Yi's fans.

Qiao Yi deeply knows that her vitality lies in creating works whole-heartedly. She has gradually become accustomed to the following netizens. However, she seems to be more indoor girl in her daily life, except that she often stays with Bai Xuan's nephew and niece, the dragon-phoenix twins when free.

Bai Xuan felt that it was time to let Qiao Yi understand his boundless dense affection for her. The two walked on the big lawn of his villa. The sky was clear, the blue waves not far away rubbed into peace, and the gentle breeze that came slowly contained a special pleasant smell of the deep sea.

Bai Xuan took advantage of Qiao Yi's unpreparedness to hold her delicate hand tightly, with the fingers interlocked. The corners of his perfect mouth brightly raised, and a charming smile appeared on his high-cold outstanding handsome face. He enjoyed watching her shyness and nervousness: "Actually, since your university graduation internship, when you often stayed at the open-air balcony of the building opposite my private office, I have noticed you sat on the bench, and since then you have entered my heart. Qiao Yi, I do need you to spend the rest of my life with me."

Qiao Yi was amazed in her heart. It turned out that they fell in love with each other silently. A soul touching smile bloomed on her vividly exquisite oval face: "Okay, we spend the rest of our life together." (End)

www.ingramcontent.com/pod-product-compliance
Lightning Source LLC
Chambersburg PA
CBHW070459200726
48293CB00007B/2299